# *ALL YOU CAN HANDLE*

*The Moments in Maplesville Series*

**Farrah Rochon**



Nicobar Press

Cover by Mae Phillips of
CoverFreshDesigns.com
Edited by Karen Dale Harris



ISBN: 978-1-938125-21-8

Dedicated to all my readers who have encouraged me to continue with the Moments in Maplesville series!

# Chapter One

The distinctive click of billiard balls crashing against each other mingled with '90s R&B music and thick southern accents, creating a discordant melody that was native to the string of dive bars that hugged this strip of the Louisiana Bayou. The Corral was just that type of bar.

Ian Landry hooked the heel of his brand new Andrew Marc shoes on the barstool's bottom rung and popped a couple of pieces of The Corral's famous spicy bar mix in his mouth. It was nothing more than Chex Mix sprinkled with Tabasco and salt, but it was tasty and it was free. Of course, the bar made its money back in the number of drinks you needed after a couple of handfuls of the peppery snack.

"What up, dawg? You ready to get this party started?"

He spun his barstool around to find his best friends, Sam Stewart and Dale Chauvin, walking up to the bar. They each clapped a hand on Ian's shoulder as they climbed up on the stools on either side of him.

Sam's grin fell as he pointed to the glass in Ian's hand.

"What the hell is that? Soda? That's what

you call celebrating?" Sam rapped his knuckles on the scarred bar top. "Hey Joe, can you get this man a real drink?"

"Don't, Joe," Ian called. "I'm good with what I have."

"Dude, come on." Sam groaned. "I thought we were celebrating? One beer won't hurt you."

And now Ian understood why Dale had called to say that he would be bringing Sam to the bar. The slight slur thickening his friend's tongue told Ian that Sam had started celebrating hours ago. If he had to guess, Ian would say he was about a drink and a half from reaching the legal limit.

"Did you get the loan pre-approval?" Dale asked. A former linebacker at LSU, his bulky frame took up more space than anyone else at the bar. "I assume that's what we're celebrating, right?"

"I won't know the amount for a few days, but I've got a damn good feeling about it," Ian said.

In fact, he felt so good about his chances of getting the loan he needed to buy the building for the motorcycle shop he'd dreamed of opening for years, that he'd texted both Sam and Dale from the bank's parking lot and told them to meet him here at the bar to celebrate. Mr. Babineaux, the loan officer at the Maplesville Savings and Loan, had given him all kinds of good vibes.

It helped that Babineaux was a bona fide motorcycle head; the man had framed pictures of his Harley and Ducati on his desk next to the one of his wife and kids. He and Ian had spent more time talking about intake valves than about Ian's credit. He'd left the bank feeling as if he could have asked for twice the purchasing power he'd requested, but he didn't need a cent over the amount he'd asked for on his mortgage loan application.

His plan was solid. He knew exactly what he needed to get his business off the ground. The key component? The old Miller's Pharmacy building in the heart of Maplesville's Historic District. The building had been vacant for years, its huge, boarded up windows just begging for a "For Sale" sign, but the Miller family had never indicated that they were willing to sell.

Then Dale's older sister, Vanessa Chauvin, who was at the pulse of Maplesville's real estate market, had gotten word that the family was finally ready to unload the property. Vanessa, who had been like a big sister to all three of them—and had labeled Dale, Sam, and Ian The Three Amigos in high school—knew Ian had his eye on that building. She'd promised to give him first crack at buying the place if it ever became available.

Ian leaned over and whispered in Dale's ear. "Vanessa is still keeping her eye out on the Miller's place for me, right?"

His friend nodded as he took a pull on his beer. "She's waiting for the property appraiser she normally works with to come back from vacation. Said the family should have the selling price nailed down within the week."

Ian planned to have the full asking price in hand when the property finally went on the market. Maplesville's population had exploded in the last few years, with new businesses and residents moving in at a rate that could give a person whiplash. Miller's Pharmacy was in the old part of town, which was beginning to reassert itself now that the monotony of the newer strip malls no longer held people's attention. These days it was all about the charm of the aged-brick storefronts and the lure of the town's quaint historic district.

Ian had a feeling that the city council had caught on to what the folks in neighboring Gauthier had accomplished. The small town, which was a quick twenty minutes east, had put itself on the map by embracing it's history and turning itself into a tourist destination.

Ian didn't care what was behind it all. He just knew he wanted in on the action. Miller's Pharmacy, with its huge windows and prime location, was the perfect spot. He needed that building.

And with Vanessa's and Richard Babineaux's help, he was going to get it.

"You guys doing alright?" Joe Poche, who'd

taken over The Corral a few years ago, asked as he wiped down the bar. "How's your dad doing, Sam?"

Sam grimaced and shrugged. And Ian knew what would come next.

"Let me have another shot," Sam said, sliding his shot glass toward the bartender.

Ian looked over at Dale. His friend's discrete nod told him that he understood what Ian was trying to say. Someone would have to get Sam home tonight. It was Dale's turn.

He wasn't sure what they were going to do about Sam, but it was becoming more apparent every time they hung out that something would have to be done. Homeboy was dancing much too close to the edge lately. Not that anyone could blame him. Watching ALS slowly steal his dad was hard for all of them. But Ian was afraid that sooner or later Sam was going to fall right off that cliff.

He didn't want to kill his good vibe thinking about the inevitable hardship they would face when Sam's dad eventually succumbed to his disease. Sam was right. Tonight was about celebrating.

Taking a sip of the ginger ale he'd been nursing for the past twenty minutes, Ian leaned back on the stool's cracked pleather and let his eyes roam around The Corral. The bar, like just about everything else in this town, played off the name of the high school mascot, the Maplesville

Mustangs. The Corral was an institution. Back when he was in high school, it was a rite of passage for the kids from Maplesville High to try and get through the door, but in a town that was once so small that practically everyone knew everyone else, it wasn't an easy feat.

He, Dale and Sam had made a promise to hang out at The Corral every weekend once they turned twenty-one, but life had gotten in the way for the three of them over the past five years. Now, they were lucky if they got together once a month. That's one of the reasons Ian had called his boys over to help him celebrate. They knew about his dream, had been a part of it since those days they used to join him and his dad in their garage; working on old bikes they'd scored from junkyards. This celebration was as much Sam and Dale's as it was his.

Ian unbuttoned a second button at his collar and wiggled it around, trying to create some space so he could breathe. He'd been so psyched following the meeting at the bank that he hadn't bothered to go home and change out of his monkey suit, which he'd bought specifically to impress Babineaux. His only other suit was the one he wore at funerals, and he didn't want to jinx the outcome of his meeting with the bank by wearing something he only wore when someone died. Ian had a feeling that this one, which had cost more than he'd ever spent on a piece of clothing, would soon be crowned his lucky suit.

Sam nudged Ian's shoulder. "Look who's over at the pool table," he said, nodding to the left side of the bar which housed several pool tables, dartboards, and an old-fashioned jukebox that hadn't worked since Bill Clinton's first term.

Several guys from St. Pierre, which had been one of their biggest rivals back during their days on the high school football field, occupied a pool table. They'd become friendly rivals after graduation, but Sam tended to forget that from time to time. Usually those times when he was getting better acquainted with his favorite drink.

"Don't go over there starting shit," Ian warned.

Sam threw back the shot of whiskey Joe had set before him. "I live to start shit." He slapped the empty shot glass on the bar and took off for the pool tables.

"This is getting worse," Dale said.

Ian released a sigh. "Can you blame him? I sure as hell can't," Ian said. "It's been nearly a decade since I lost my dad and I'm still not over it. It can't be easy for him to watch his slowly dying."

"Yeah, well, call me crazy, but I don't see how starting shit with those guys from St. Pierre helps anything," Dale countered.

Ian agreed. He just hoped that tonight didn't end with Joe calling the cops.

He twirled his stool around, but stopped mid-twist as his gaze landed on the woman sitting on the other side of the bar. His breath skidded to a stop in his lungs and his heart skipped several beats before it started pumping again.

The wild, crazy Afro was the first thing that snagged his attention, but it took only seconds before Ian's brain registered the rest of her. Satiny, rich umber skin draped over the most gorgeous cheekbones he'd ever seen. No, gorgeous didn't do her justice.

Flawless. That was a better word.

"Shit, I need to go over there and make sure Sam doesn't get into trouble," Dale said as he climbed down from the barstool. "You coming?"

"Nah, I'm good right here." Ian took another sip of his soda, his eyes not leaving the beauty at the bar. For a moment he'd forgotten that his two best friends even existed. His sole focus was on the gorgeous stranger.

Maplesville had grown over the last few years, with new businesses and apartment complexes popping up like zits on a teenager's forehead. It wasn't as easy to keep track of the new people strolling into town. The beauty sitting at the bar was definitely new to the area. She wasn't the kind of woman you stood behind in the line at the grocery store and then forgot about while putting away your frozen pizzas. If Ian had ever seen her around town before, he would have remembered.

Her fingers tapped on the bar top in rhythm

with the music, but after receiving her drink, she twirled her stool around and faced the small dance floor, where about a dozen people were doing a line dance to the "Cupid Shuffle."

Her slim, delicately muscled shoulders rocked to the up-tempo beat. They were bare, the tail end of her sleeveless button-down shirt tied in a knot just below her breasts, exposing an expanse of smooth, dark brown skin that made Ian's pulse quicken.

Huge, thin hoops hung from her ears. She had at least twenty gold bangles around her wrist, going nearly halfway up her arm, and every one of her fingers had a ring on it, her thumbs included. It was hard to see from this distance, but Ian thought he could make out a small stud in her nose.

He wasn't sure if it was a tattoo he saw peeking out of the waistband of her skin-tight dark blue jeans, or if it was just the dim lighting in The Corral playing tricks on his eyes, but he liked the thought of it. A mysterious tattoo on a mysterious woman. A stunningly gorgeous mysterious woman.

He was tempted to take a discrete snapshot of her with his phone, but that shit was creepy, and he was too afraid someone would catch him in the act. Better to just commit that face to memory.

All of a sudden she turned and looked directly at him.

Ian's first instinct was to avert his eyes, pretend he hadn't been staring at her. But he was feeling confident after his meeting at the bank. Add in the new suit and the wink he'd received earlier today when he'd run into Naomi Elliot—the girl every boy had coveted back in junior high—and Ian might as well draw an S on his chest. Make that an H and an S for Hot Shit. Because that's what he was right now.

Instead of pretending he hadn't seen her, Ian tipped his glass toward the beauty with the banging Afro and nodded. She continued to stare at him, her expression giving him nothing. Maybe he wasn't the hot shit he thought he was.

He was two seconds from searching for a hole in the floor to swallow him when a subtle smile drew across her lips. She tilted her beer bottle toward him.

Oh, yeah. Hell yeah.

But then she turned her attention back to the dance floor. Ian waited for her to look his way, but two songs played over the bar's loud sound system and not once did those dark eyes return to his side of the bar.

He considered walking over there, but that wave of confidence he'd been riding had begun to drift back down to the shore. After the string of home runs he'd hit today, Ian didn't want to end it by striking out with the beauty across the bar.

Instead, he dropped a five on the bar for Joe

and joined Sam and Dale at the pool table.

Sonny White observed the small crowd moving in step with each other on the scuffed dance floor. Some were pretty good, but some of them were downright awful. For a brief moment she considered joining them, but a dancer she was not.

Besides, Sonny wasn't particularly keen on looking like a fool in front of that cute honey drop who'd been sitting at the other end of the bar. He'd moved over to the pool table, where his rowdy friend with the high-top fade circa 1991 was talking loud enough for the entire bar to hear him. She felt sorry for the poor little train wreck. He was so drunk Sonny was sure he'd have to be carried out of the bar.

The honey drop, along with the other one she'd labeled The Hulk, kept a close watch on Drunk Boy. Yet, Honey Drop's eyes continued to dart her way every few minutes. It was both adorable and nerve-racking.

She'd been watching him from the corner of her eye for nearly a half hour. It had taken him long enough to notice her, but apparently, he was too clueless to realize that he should be over here offering to buy her a drink instead of babysitting his drunk friend. It looked as if she would have to make the first move.

But she didn't.

She was still trying to decide if she was the kind of girl who was capable of picking up a guy in a bar. She'd been stalwart in her effort to embrace this new, more carefree lifestyle she'd embarked upon, but some actions still gave her pause. Like walking up to a cute guy in a bar and introducing herself.

Besides, she still wasn't sure if he was worth it. His nicely cut suit and shiny wingtips were a solid knock against him. The stuffy attire was too reminiscent of Douglas Edwards, III—the mistake she'd nearly married after a five-year relationship. Goodness, she needed another drink just to wash that thought out of her head.

On the other hand, maybe the fact that he reminded her of her ex wasn't such a bad thing. If the cute little morsel trying his hardest not to stare at her was nothing more than Douglas 2.0, Sonny had very little chance of falling for him. And, let's be honest, she was not picking up some guy in a bar in hopes of finding life-long love. If she went over there, it would be with one goal in mind.

She wanted to get laid. God, did she want to get laid.

But there were other factors to consider. For one thing, she was new to this area. Even though she wasn't planning to stay in this town for very long, she still needed to be mindful of her actions. She wasn't sure how one-night stands worked in Small Town, USA. Was Maplesville big enough for her to have some naked fun with the Honey Drop tonight and then not see him again? Or was she setting herself up for awkward encounters at the post office?

Wait! When was the last time she'd physically mailed anything?

Decision made, Sonny downed the remainder of her gin and tonic in one swallow and hopped off the barstool. Tugging up the waistband of her snug, low-riding jeans, she headed for the pool table, moving with a confidence she'd always possessed, but had never been comfortable showing.

That was something that was gradually changing, too.

With every day that passed she became a bit more comfortable embracing the Sonny she'd suppressed all of these years. It was liberating as hell.

She wasn't sure if picking up a guy in a bar counted as another move in the Emancipation of Sonny movement, or if it was just plain stupid, but she was slightly buzzed from her drink and riding high off the excitement of the job she'd accepted today with a local catering company. It seemed like the perfect ending to her day.

Sonny hadn't anticipated her journey bringing her to a small town like Maplesville, but she wasn't questioning it, either. She'd taken her future into her own hands, doing what would make her happy, instead of living her life for her parents and ex-fiancé.

And she had a feeling that the cutie in the charcoal-grey pinstripe could make her very happy. At least for tonight.

Sonny walked up to the pool table and shoved both hands in her back pockets so that her breasts would thrust forward at just the right angle. She wedged herself between him and the pool table, blocking the shot he was about to take.

"I'm Madison," she said.

His eyes went wide, as if she'd caught him completely off guard. As if she hadn't seen the way he'd tracked her out of the corner of his eye the entire way there.

Oh, the Honey Drop was adorable. And younger than she'd first thought. He couldn't be older than her own twenty-eight years.

His hair was cut close, and it waved in short ripples. A fine sheen of sweat pebbled along the edge of his forehead, making his light brown skin glisten. He had a set of the most beautiful eyes she'd ever seen, a soft, amber-green rimmed with gold. Gorgeous. Heart-stopping even.

Yeah, she could do this. She could be the kind of girl who made the first move.

"Ian," he said, setting his pool cue to the side and stretching a palm toward her.

Sonny looked down at his hand and allowed

a small smile to curl up the edges of her mouth before taking the hand he offered. His palm was surprisingly rough, much rougher than she'd expected from a guy wearing a suit like this one.

She gestured toward the pool table. "Are you winning?"

"No."

"Good. Then you shouldn't feel bad about abandoning the game so you can dance with me. Unless you have to stay here and babysit your friend." She tipped her head toward the loudmouth, who'd just gotten up in one of the other player's faces. That would not end well.

Ian shook his head. "He's probably going to get his ass kicked, so that would be a no on the babysitting front. However, I still can't do what you suggested."

Her newly minted self-confidence took a slight hit, until he leaned forward and whispered in her ear, "I don't dance."

Sonny's smile widened. "Neither do I. But I'm sure we can find something else to do."

Whoa. Who was this woman hitting it out of the park in the brave and sexy department?

With boldness practically oozing from her pores, Sonny led him to the only available booth remaining in the bar, which had swelled with patrons over the past hour. She hadn't expected such a crowd on a Monday night, but apparently this was how they rolled in small towns like Maplesville.

When Ian made a move to sit opposite of her, she tugged on his cuff, pulling him into the booth next to her. She twisted on the worn maroon Naugahyde and bent one leg to prop her sandal-clad foot up on the bench. The gold from her favorite toe ring gleamed under the lights. She set her elbow on the tabletop and rested her chin on her fist.

"It sure took you long enough to notice me," Sonny opened. "I've been sitting over there trying to snag your attention for nearly an hour."

"Have you?"

"Don't bullshit me," she said. "You've been watching me all night. I just said that to stroke your ego."

He chuckled. "Okay, so maybe I've been watching you too. I've been trying to figure out those mixed signals you've been tossing my way."

She released an exaggerated gasp. "Mixed signals? I have not been sending you any such thing."

"Yeah, yeah, yeah," he drawled, his eyes dancing with amusement. "You can save that drama for the stage. I'm not buying the innocent act."

"I wasn't acting," Sonny said. She traced her finger along the rim of the table. "I was trying to decide if you were worth it."

A curious brow peaked over those gorgeous

amber-green eyes. "And?"

His voice had dipped several octaves, making her skin tingle with that single word.

Sonny matched his raised brow. "We're sitting here together, aren't we?"

A slow smile stretched across his lips, and for the first time she noticed the small dimple in his cheek. Just like that, she was toast. Resisting that dimple was out of the question.

Sonny lost track of time as minutes meandered into hours. Their conversation spanned the entire spectrum of ridiculousness, from arguing over the casting in the Marvel Comics action movies, to agreeing on the brilliance of McDonald's perennial McRib. She'd never imagined there could be so many double entendres about a sandwich.

With every sexy, flirty innuendo that passed her lips, the fake, cloistered Madison White she'd been molded into over the course of her life died a little more. She felt emboldened; the wild and free Sonny she'd embraced didn't hesitate when it came to asking for what she wanted.

And right now, she wanted Ian.

"So, why don't you dance?" she asked him.

He shrugged. "Just not my thing. Why don't you?"

"Because I look like a drowning duck whenever I try to dance," she said with a laugh. "Even years of classes couldn't help me. I'm living proof that the 'all black people can dance' stereotype is just a myth."

"You can't be that bad."

"You wanna bet?" She asked. She tipped her head back and downed the remainder of the drink she'd been nursing for the past half-hour, then grabbed Ian by the wrist.

He tugged. "What are you doing?"

"Come on," she said. "I demand we get on the dance floor and make fools of ourselves."

Pulling him out of the booth, she grabbed him by the lapels of that nice-fitting suit and didn't stop until they were smack in the center of the dance floor.

She didn't worry about learning the dance moves. She could get what she wanted by simply moving her hips from side to side. She turned around and fitted her back against his front, pulling Ian's right hand around her waist and placing it over her bellybutton. He flicked his thumb back and forth over her bellybutton ring.

"This is so damn sexy," he whispered in her ear.

Taking full control of the brazenness she'd been cultivating over the course of the evening, she rubbed her backside against him and was rewarded moments later with the reaction she'd hoped for. The telltale bulge that hardened behind his zipper spurred her on, feeding her self-confidence, daring her to be bolder than she ever thought she could be. She ground herself even more against him, her stomach fluttering at the desperate moan he made in her ear.

"You okay back there?" Sonny asked over her shoulder.

He answered with a deep chuckle, the rumble cascading down her spine.

She swayed her hips again. "Just let me know if there's anything I can help you with."

His other hand came around her waist, his fingers locking just above the snap of her jeans.

"What are you offering?" he asked.

His hips undulated the slightest bit, his erection fitting against her backside.

Her blood quickened, a mixture of apprehension and anticipation shooting through her veins. Sonny looked back and pulled her bottom lip between her teeth. Ian's eyes dropped to her mouth as he released a slow breath. She turned in his arms, so that his clasped hands now rested at the small of her back.

She looked up at Ian and was nearly singed by the heat in his eyes. There was no doubt about what he wanted.

This was it. Decision time. The moment was hers for the taking.

How far was she ready to take this bold new Sonny? Far enough to sleep with a complete stranger?

No.

She was bold, but she wasn't that bold just

yet.

Sonny's mouth dipped in an apologetic frown. "I think maybe we should stick to dancing."

In that moment she loathed herself. She hated that she'd uttered those words, but Sonny knew she would hate herself even more if she'd said anything else. Embracing this new Sonny was a gradual process. She just wasn't there yet.

Dammit.

"It's okay," Ian whispered. "I understand." Sonny's eyes flew to his. He nodded. "I do," he said.

After her heavy flirting, a lot of other guys would have accused her of leading them on. For the barest second Sonny reconsidered, but she knew she couldn't go through with it. What if she did have to mail off a package one of these days and ran into him at the post office? Or the grocery store? Or the dry cleaners? Talk about awkward.

She didn't want to introduce any drama into her life, and trying to avoid seeing her one-night stand around town would be unnecessary drama.

She reached behind her and pulled his hands from where they rested at the small of her back. "It's probably time for me to get out of here," she said.

"You sure?"

She nodded.

"Okay, then. I'll walk you to your car," he said. He must have noticed the caution that flashed in her eyes because he followed with, "I swear, I just want to walk you to your car. I won't try anything with you."

Could he really be as sweet as he seemed? Maybe this didn't have to be one night…

Sonny tossed that idea out of her head. The one thing she was definitely not looking for was a commitment of any kind. She'd just broken free from five years of captivity. The last thing she needed was to be shackled to someone again.

At least this way, if she did happen to run into Ian during her short stint in Maplesville, there would be none of that uncomfortable small talk that she suspected happened when virtual strangers, who just happened to know what the other looked like naked, encountered each other again. That was the one bright spot to not taking tonight any farther than they'd already taken it.

A genuine smile lifted the corners of her mouth. "Yes," she answered. "I'd like it very much if you were to walk me to my car."

Taking him by the hand, they made their way off the dance floor and through the bar's double doors. Ian's friends had left over an hour ago, The Hulk, whom he'd introduced as Dale, had to help the other friend, Sam, out of the bar.

"I'm parked over there," Sonny said, pointing towards the graveled parking lot to the right side of the building. The number of cars crowding the lot had thinned considerably since she'd first arrived. Her vintage VW Bug sat nearly hidden against the seven-foot-tall wooden fence, the branches of an oak tree on the other side of the fence reaching over to create a canopy for her car.

"That your car?" Ian asked, speeding up his steps. He let go of her hand as he rounded her VW. "What year is this? Looks like a '62."

"You know your cars," Sonny said.

"This is a classic. You buy it already restored, or did you have it done?"

"It was a rusty pile of junk when I bought it," she said.

"No kidding?" He looked up at her. "Original engine?"

Sonny nodded.

He let out a low whistle as he peered inside the car through the driver's side window. "Can't be easy finding parts for this baby."

"It's a nightmare." She laughed. "I had no idea it would be so ridiculously expensive to maintain, but I love it." Sonny walked over and unlocked the driver's side door. "Get in," she said.

He looked up at her again. "You sure?"

She nodded. "I can tell how much you want to see it."

His lips quirked. "Now, if we're talking about what I really want to see..."

A coy smile drew across her lips.

"It's not what you think," he said. He tipped his head toward the rear of the car.

Sonny thought for a moment then burst out laughing. She went around to the back of the car and lifted the latch on the rear engine.

"Oh wow," Ian said. He reached for the engine, then pulled his hand back. "Can I?"

"Go ahead." She loved the pure awe in his voice. Anyone who could appreciate a classic VW Bug was gold in her eyes.

Ian placed his palm on the camshaft and released a deep moan. "This makes up for no sex."

Her head flew back with her laugh.

"I'm serious," Ian said. "This is like touching history. Not that touching you wouldn't have been historic, but this…this is a '62 Beetle."

"You're actually comparing sex with me to touching my car?"

"I should stop while I'm ahead, shouldn't I?"

"I think so," Sonny said, laughing again. She couldn't help it. He was way too adorable. And sexy. And funny.

A pall stretched over her at the thought of leaving him, and she suddenly could think of nothing more than extending their time together.

"Do you want to see the inside?" Sonny asked.

His eager nod wrenched another laugh from

her. He ran over to the driver's side and got in.

Sonny lifted the duffle bag from the passenger-side floorboard and tossed it in the backseat with her other luggage before getting in the car.

Ian sat behind the wheel, caressing the restored leather steering wheel with a reverence reserved for historical relics. They switched sides, with Sonny getting behind the wheel while Ian checked things out from the passenger side.

She thought about Douglas's reaction when she told him she wanted to buy this car. He'd called her ridiculous and told her—no demanded—that she get a car more suitable for a grown woman.

How could she have compared Ian to Douglas? Attire aside, they were nothing alike. Sonny could tell after just a few hours with him.

Ian ran his hand along the dash, and then he caressed the inside of the door. Sonny's skin tingled with the need to have him do the same to her.

"It's nice to find someone who appreciates a classic when he sees it," she said.

He looked over at her. The searing heat in his hooded eyes was enough to scorch her. If her body wasn't burning hot already.

"I know a good thing when I see one," he said.

She pulled in a breath and let it out with a

rush. "Do you now?"

Ian nodded. The desire that pulsed between them was a living, breathing thing, occupying every available space within the small confines of the car.

To hell with awkward moments at the post office. After a lifetime of playing it safe, she was ready to be a little reckless.

Sonny climbed over the gearshift and straddled his lap, attacking his mouth with a desperation she'd never experienced before. Stripping his jacket off, she dove for Ian's neck, sucking just under his jaw.

He reached up and turned the interior light off. She hated that he did—she wanted to see him—but she knew it was better, just in case someone entered the parking lot. The tree branches provided some shelter, but not enough to shield them completely.

His hands caught her at the waist and started to run up and down her spine with the same reverence he'd shown to the car's interior. He brought his hands to the front and untied the knot under her breasts. His fingers trembled as he undid the buttons of her shirt.

When he spread the shirt open, he released a moan.

"How did I not realize you weren't wearing a bra?" he asked. He leaned forward and sucked her nipple into his mouth.

Sonny's head pitched back as she cradled his

head between her palms and held him to her aching breasts.

"Are you sure about this?" Ian asked.

"Are you carrying a condom?" she panted. He nodded. "Then I'm sure."

The awkwardness of the narrow space did nothing to detract from the heat pulsating between them. She lifted from his lap and unzipped her jeans. As she worked the tight denim over her hips, Ian pulled a condom from his wallet, opened the fly of his pants and pulled out a frighteningly hard erection.

"That must have been uncomfortable," she said.

"I've been dying here," Ian said. He covered himself with the condom, captured her hips, and brought her down on his hardness.

Sonny bit her lip to stop herself from screaming with pleasure. With her shirt still on but the front open to him, she rode his lap with fevered strokes. Ian's mouth went from one breast to the other, his tongue and teeth whipping her into a frenzy.

It was raw and rough, this meeting of their bodies, and it was exactly what she needed. Sonny lost herself in the sensation of his solid length penetrating her. Every desperate grunt that escaped Ian's mouth urged her on. She gripped his shoulders, using him to leverage her up and down, her pace increasing.

Her stomach tightened as all-consuming

pleasure gripped her. Ian's hands found her ass, his fingers digging into her tender flesh as he clutched her backside and held her down against him. His hips worked like a piston, pumping up and down in rapid succession.

Pleasure tore through her as her body went up in flames.

Even as the orgasm rippled through her body, Sonny felt another building within her belly. In seconds the pleasure erupted again, with Ian joining her this time. He growled against her, his mouth clamping on her nipple as her inner muscles milked his erection.

She collapsed against his chest, her breaths coming in shallow pants. Sonny stole a few moments to collect her breath and savor the feeling of him inside of her before lifting her body off of him.

"That was...mind-blowing," she said.

"Made me forget all about touching your engine."

Sonny laughed against his chest. "God, you're such a charmer." She pushed back and stared at him. "Not that it should matter, but I don't want you to think I do things like this all the time. In fact, I never do things like this. You're my first ever one-night stand."

"So, that's what this was?" Ian asked. "A one time thing?"

She nodded. "Yes." It had to be.

She'd had one thing in mind when she came

to this bar tonight, to let her hair down and have a little fun. And once she spotted him, her definition of fun had become a bit clearer. But this was as far as she was willing to let it go.

"I know this is a small town," Sonny continued. "But I'm hoping Maplesville is big enough for us not to run into each other."

"It can be," he said. "If that's what you want."

"I'm new here, Ian. And I don't expect to be in Maplesville for very long. You can turn into a complication I don't need."

He shoved his fingers into her hair at the base of her head, massaging her scalp. "Or I can be your new best friend who shows you around town and gives you regular orgasms."

She laughed even as a delicious shudder rolled through her at the thought. "I think I'll have to pass."

Ian released a deep breath, along with her head. He lifted a couple of fast food napkins from the stow away rack mounted behind the gearshift and used them to clean up the mess from the condom. Sonny's skin grew tight with the awkwardness suddenly suffusing the confines of the car. This was one byproduct of her boldness she hadn't foreseen.

Fitting himself back into his pants, Ian pulled up the zipper and straightened his shirt. He looked over at her and said, "I guess this is goodbye, then."

Sonny nodded, pulling her bottom lip between her teeth. Ian's fingers went to her mouth. He stroked her lips, gently tugging it free from her teeth.

"Please don't do that. You do that and it just makes me want another taste."

She went liquid again. She wanted another taste just as badly as he did, which is why she needed to end this right now.

Leaning down, she pressed a kiss to his lips. "Thank you for tonight. It's exactly the kind of welcome I needed."

"Are you sure tonight will be enough?"

"Yes. We should end this right here. It's for the best."

Ian's sigh matched hers. "If that's really what you want," he said. He cupped her cheek, his thumb caressing her skin. "Take care of this car."

Sonny laughed. "Your concern over my car is touching. And weird."

"Well, I don't have to tell you to take care of yourself. I have a feeling you know how to do that already."

He stroked his thumb along her jawline once more before pulling her head closer and capturing her lips in a slow, deep kiss. "But, just in case, take care of yourself," he said. He kissed her again, then opened the door and slid from underneath her.

Sonny pulled her jeans over her hips and

of what she had fit in the backseat of her car, although she also had a couple of boxes of items she couldn't part with stored in the tiny bedroom she'd been staying in at her old college roommate's house in Baton Rouge. If all went well, Sonny would soon be able to get her things from Karen's and bring them to her new crib.

She needed all to go well because she *needed* this apartment. In addition to being fully furnished, this place was less than a ten-minute drive to Catering by Kiera, the local catering company where tomorrow she would start as the new pastry chef. She and the owner, Kiera Coleman-Watson, had agreed to a trial run, which suited Sonny just fine. The thought of being tied down in a job—even one she liked—made Sonny's skin crawl. She needed flexibility, to know that freedom wasn't far out of reach.

And it was that flexibility that was, by far, the apartment's biggest draw. It was the only one she could find in Maplesville that offered a month-to-month lease.

Shutting off the ignition, Sonny got out of the car and walked up the walkway leading to the porch. It was cozy and quaint, with two white wooden rockers on either side of the door. The rockers seemed like a requisite for this kind of house. The Society of French Colonials would probably levy a fine on anyone who didn't put white wooden rockers on their porches.

She rang the doorbell and took a step back,

looking both left and right off the side of the porch at the pink and white begonias flourishing on either side of the house. Her mother called begonias the landscaper's friend, because they were so easy to maintain.

The front door opened and Sonny lost her ability to breathe.

"Madison?"

"Ian?"

For a second she was certain Candid Camera would jump from behind the huge azalea bush on the right side of the porch.

*This could* not *be happening*.

"What are you doing here?" Ian asked, stepping out onto the porch.

Sonny held up her phone. "Answering an ad from Craigslist. Yesterday I set up an appointment with someone named Vanessa Chauvin to see the garage apartment at this address."

His amber-green eyes went wide. "Vanessa couldn't make it, so I told her I'd show the apartment myself."

"*You* own the apartment?"

"You're the person who answered the ad? Vanessa said the renter's name was Sonny."

"Yes. *I'm* Sonny. That's my nickname. There are only a few people who call me Madison anymore."

Ian took a step back, as if he'd had the wind knocked out of him a second time. "So, you pulled the old fake name trick last night, huh?"

"I didn't give you a fake name. Madison *is* my name, but I go by Sonny."

He ran his hand over his head and down his face, then released an uneasy laugh. "This is crazy," he said. "You're here to see the apartment."

God, this really was happening.

Sonny's first instinct was to do an about-face and hightail it off of the porch, but she wanted this apartment. She *needed* this apartment.

They were adults. They would just have to deal.

"Look, Ian, this doesn't have to be weird. We can just pretend last night never happened and start fresh."

She held out her hand.

His eyes traveled from her hand up to her eyes, and a current of desire flashed through her. Less than twelve hours ago those ridiculously sexy eyes had stared at her, drenched in desire as his rock hard body penetrated her over and over again. Pretending last night didn't happen was an exercise in futility, but one she was willing to endure if it meant getting this apartment.

"You really think that's possible?" he asked. "Pretending last night never happened?"

"It is if we try hard enough."

With a subtle huff of laughter, Ian finally clasped her outstretched hand. Electricity pulsed between them. He felt it, too. Sonny could tell by the way he flexed his fingers once he released her hand, as if he was trying to shake off the effects of their skin meeting again.

Yeah, pretending last night never happened probably wouldn't work.

"Of course, if we can avoid being seen by the neighbors I guess we can occasionally give in to the temptation of sneaking into each other's rooms at night," Sonny said with a nervous laugh.

Instead of answering with the suggestive reply she anticipated, Ian remained silent. His brow furrowed slightly.

*Okay. Apparently* someone *couldn't take a joke.*

Sonny cleared her throat. "Can I see the apartment?"

Several heartbeats passed before he nodded and took a step back.

"Yeah, sure. Of course." He gestured for her to enter the house ahead of him. "Let me just get the key."

She stepped into the brief foyer that led into an open living room and dining room area, separated by three white columns. The house was beautiful. A bit messy, with several pairs of tennis shoes kicked off haphazardly next to the sofa, magazines scattered on the end table, and a jacket tossed in a chair. But it was tastefully decorated and had the kind of live-in feel that the cavernous mansion she'd grown up in could never attain.

Ian appeared in the short hallway, keys dangling from his finger, and motioned for her to follow him. "Let's go through the kitchen. It's easier to get to the garage."

Sonny swallowed her envious sigh as she followed him through the kitchen. The massive amount of counter space was a pastry chef's wet dream. The center island boasted a single sink with a towering gooseneck faucet. Cast-iron pots and pans hung from a rack above it. She wondered if they were just for show or if Ian actually cooked.

Sonny was suddenly struck by the absurdity of this entire situation. She knew how his eyes fluttered closed when he orgasmed, but she didn't know if he liked to cook.

Why did she think a one-night stand wouldn't be a big deal?

She decided to cut herself some slack. She could not possibly have guessed that the one guy in Maplesville whom she'd allowed herself to sleep with would turn out to be her potential landlord. She knew this town was small but she couldn't have ever anticipated it being *this* small.

Ian led her across the driveway to the garage, which they entered through a side door. Instead of a car, there were at least a half-dozen motorcycles occupying the space. Two were covered with light brown tarps. Several others lay on their sides, parts strewn about them on the garage floor. The last one—a huge, gleaming machine of polished black and chrome—sat uncovered in the middle of the space.

"You like bikes," Sonny observed.

Ian looked over his shoulder at the collection of motorcycles. "Yeah," was all he said.

She stopped short, her spine stiffening with affront.

She didn't know what to make of his terse responses. It was as if he'd become an entirely different person after her off-hand suggestion about sneaking into each other's rooms. Maybe she should clarify that it was just a joke?

Okay, so maybe there'd been a touch of truth to it when she'd suggested it, but Sonny would never admit to that now. Not with the way he'd reacted. This aloof, unapproachable person he'd turned into following her joke was so different from the guy she'd met last night.

He started up the interior steps leading to the apartment, but Sonny stopped him, grabbing his wrist. He looked down at where she held him. She waited until his eyes met hers again before she spoke.

"Ian, let me know if this is too awkward for you. I'm really interested in this apartment—there are a number of reasons why it is absolutely perfect for me—but if this is too uncomfortable for you I'll understand."

He hesitated for a moment before shaking his head. "No, we're good," he said, and continued up the stairs.

She wasn't sure how much she believed that, but if that's what he needed to tell himself to make this okay, so be it.

The stairs led directly into the studio apartment. The moment she entered the space, Sonny knew this was exactly where she wanted to live.

It was more spacious than she'd anticipated, with two large windows overlooking the driveway, allowing ample natural sunlight to flood the apartment. A small kitchen was tucked into the back right corner; equipped with a two-burner stove, single sink, microwave and full-sized refrigerator.

"There's not much to it," Ian said. He pointed to the door directly across from them. "There's the bathroom. There isn't a full-size tub, only a shower." He pointed to a red and black Chinese screen. "There's a twin bed behind there. It isn't all that comfortable from what I can recall. There's also a closet over there," he said, gesturing to the left side across from the kitchen.

If this was how he typically presented the apartment to perspective tenants, it was no wonder this place was still vacant. Sonny could only hope that the real estate agent who was supposed to show her the apartment had a better spiel.

"Vanessa Chauvin mentioned that utilities are paid," Sonny said.

He nodded. "Yeah, they are. It's also wired for cable, but I've got satellite in the house. You would have to call the cable company and have them reconnect the service if you want it."

"Internet?"

"I don't have any trouble connecting wirelessly when I'm working in the garage. I'm pretty sure you'll be able to get online up here. You'll just need the password to the network."

"Do you work in the garage often?" she asked.

The idea of walking downstairs and finding Ian sweaty and covered in sawdust or motor oil or whatever gave men that earthy smell after working all day with their hands made her lightheaded.

"I'm down there a lot," he answered. "I restore bikes in my spare time."

She nodded and pulled her bottom lip between her teeth.

"Will that be a problem?" he asked.

"No." She shook her head a bit too emphatically.

He shoved his hands in his front jean pockets and lifted his shoulders in a hapless shrug. "Okay. Well, feel free to look around for a while. Make sure it's exactly what you want."

Sonny heard the sound of the door downstairs opening moments before footsteps pounded up the stairs.

"Hey Ian, I need your help."

A young girl with long, skinny micro braids stopped short as she arrived at the top of the stairs.

"Oh. Hey," she said. She turned to Ian. "The switch isn't working on my robot. I need you to see what's going on with it."

"In a minute, Kimmie," Ian said.

Sonny just stared. The girl, who looked to be about eleven or twelve, was a female version of Ian, with those remarkable eyes and golden brown skin.

Was this his daughter?

Sonny had to remind herself to take a breath.

"Uh, this is my younger sister, Kimberlyn. Kimmie, this is Madison…uhh…Sonny. She's thinking about renting the apartment."

Kimberlyn walked up to her with wide-eyed fascination. "I love your hair," she said, reaching up to touch Sonny's 'fro before jerking her hand back.

"Come on," Ian said, clamping a hand on his little sister's shoulder. He turned to Sonny. "Look around and let me know if you have any questions. I'll be back in a few minutes."

Sonny swallowed then nodded. "Okay, thanks. Nice to meet you, Kimmie."

"You, too," the girl said. "Oh, and this place is really cool. You'll like it. You should stay."

Sonny smiled at the little girl's enthusiasm, but she still wasn't sure what to make of Ian's oddly cold reception.

She would have expected that type of reaction from the guy in the stuffy suit, yet last night he'd been the epitome of laid back and fun. It was today, dressed in sweatpants and a t-shirt that showed off just the right amount of his toned chest, that he came across as aloof and uptight.

She shook her head. Figuring out Ian should be the least of her worries. She wasn't here to figure him out; she was here for this apartment. That's what she should be concentrating on.

Sonny meandered around the space for a bit, but it didn't take long to confirm her initial expectation. This place was perfect for her. The only thing that wasn't clear was whether or not she could handle living so close to her new landlord.

"I don't know what happened. It was working just fine yesterday, but today?" Kimmie lifted her shoulders in a hapless shrug. "Fix it. Please!"

Ian sat at the dining room table, which was covered in various electronics. He took the robot he and his twelve-year-old sister had built over the course of the last three weeks and peered inside, hoping he could spot the issue without having to open the acrylic body casing.

Actually, having to break open the body

casing wouldn't be a bad thing. It would give him an excuse to stay away from the garage apartment. He needed some time to think before he faced Madison—*Sonny*—again.

"Please don't tell me it's broken," Kimmie said.

"Give me a minute to look at it," Ian said.

Kimmie was convinced that most of her classmates in the science and technology category at this year's science fair would be doing something pertaining to the Internet or telecommunications. She wanted to go "old school" and work with animatronics. Being a bona fide gear-head, Ian had been geeked with her choice. He may have had more fun working on the science fair project than Kimmie had.

"Everything looks good from here," Ian said, twisting the robot around in his hands. "You're sure it's fully charged?"

"It's been on the charger all night."

"If that's the case than it should have enough juice to stay powered for at least—" Ian stopped short as he looked at the small round side table where the charger sat. "Umm, Kimmie," he said, walking over to the table. He picked up the cord, which dangled over the edge. "Was the charger itself plugged into the outlet?"

Kimmie's mouth dropped open. "I...thought so."

Grinning, Ian plugged the charger into the

wall socket and then plugged the robot into the charger. It lit up, its arms moving up and down, its square head turning from left to right.

"Yes, yes, yes!" Kimmie pumped her fist in the air, then dashed over to him and lifted the robot from his fingers. "Now I can shoot my next scene."

Ian folded his arms across his chest. "I thought we agreed that you wouldn't shoot your movie until after the science fair?"

"These are just practice scenes," she said as she fiddled with the Sony Action Cam handheld video camera Ian had bought her for Christmas.

He knew he should order her to get back to learning her information for the science fair, but Ian decided to leave her to her movie making for now. Even though *he* thought building a robot was the coolest thing on the face of the earth, Kimmie was more concerned with making them the stars of her next big feature film. His baby sister was determined to take Hollywood by storm. She just had to get through junior high first.

Ian made his way back to the kitchen. He stopped with his hand on the door, his head falling forward as he sucked in a deep breath. He wasn't ready to go back into the garage.

Was it the coincidence to top all coincidences, or was it just his bad luck that the woman who had occupied every square centimeter of his brain since she'd pulled out of the parking lot of The Corral last night would be the same person who Vanessa had described as the *perfect* candidate to rent his garage apartment?

Coincidence or not, the question was what exactly was he going to do about it?

When he'd opened his front door and saw her standing there, it was like a dream come to life. Until she mentioned sneaking into his room. Then he remembered the young, impressionable pre-teen who slept just down the hallway from him.

That's when Ian realized how so very dangerous it would be to have the woman he'd spent the night fantasizing about living just a few yards away.

A part of him wanted to tell her that the apartment was no longer available. He could say that he and Vanessa had gotten their wires crossed and the apartment had been promised to someone else.

But what would he say if, in a few weeks, she discovered there was no one living there? In a town as small as Maplesville, it wasn't unreasonable to assume that word wouldn't get back to her.

Besides, he needed to get this apartment rented out as soon as possible. He'd already listed it as extra income on his loan application. Mr. Babineaux at the bank had encouraged him to provide as many income streams as possible, suggesting that it made Ian a more attractive candidate for a mortgage.

Ian had been hesitant, because finding a renter had not been the easiest task, especially with all the new apartment complexes coming up in town. It's why he'd enlisted Vanessa's help. When he'd tried renting it out on his own, the only takers Ian had found were a loner with bloodshot eyes and a college kid whose clothes reeked of marijuana. He had to be picky when it came to choosing a renter. He wouldn't have just anyone living so close to Kimmie.

It wasn't as if he knew Sonny all that well, but hell, he'd had sex with her in a Volkswagen. That had to count for something.

It was the *something* that made him edgy.

If circumstances were different he would jump at the chance to have Sonny living just steps away from him, but he had to consider the kind of influence his actions had on Kimmie.

There was a knock on the kitchen door. Ian looked up and let out a soft groan at the sight of the wild Afro silhouetted behind the burnt orange curtains. His fingers were itching to sink into that 'fro again. To hold her head steady as she rode him hard and fast…

*Shit!*

He could *not* entertain thoughts like this with his baby sister only one room away.

He sucked in a deep breath and opened the door. Sonny remained on the other side of the threshold.

"Um, you mind if I come in?" she asked.

"Oh, yeah, sure." He moved out of the doorway so that she could enter. "Sorry about that."

"It's okay," she said as she moved passed him. Her unique scent wafted through his nostrils and his body stirred to life. Goodness. Just being in the same room with this woman set his blood on fire.

Sonny walked over to the kitchen island in the center of the room.

Ian debated feeding her the mysterious other renter story for a half second before tossing the idea out.

"So, what do you think?" he asked.

She clasped her hands together and stretched them out in front of her before letting them fall back to her thighs. "It's perfect," she said. "It really is. It's just enough space, it's close to work, and it's within my budget. It's exactly what I was looking for."

Great. There was no way he could tell her no now, not with the excitement glittering in her eyes.

"Good." Ian nodded. "Yeah…that's good."

Kimmie swept into the kitchen, robot in one hand, video camera in the other. She charged up to Madison like a bull on a wavy red flag.

"So, are you staying?" Kimmie asked. "I hope you do. But I want to move into the garage when I'm sixteen, so you'd have to be out in three years. By the way, this is my robot, Fitzgerald. I call him Fitz, for short. I built him for my science project. Well, technically, Ian built him, but I helped a lot and I know exactly how he works so when it's time to present him at the science fair, no one will know that I didn't *actually* build him. So, are you going to rent the apartment?"

Sonny's face held the shell-shocked expression Ian had grown used to seeing on anyone who encountered Kimmie for the first time.

"Uh, I would like to," Sonny said.

"Awesome. If you do, can I please, please, *please* borrow those bangles? Those are in now. When I say 'in' I mean that they're in-style. It's like when old stuff becomes popular again. And those are—"

"Kimberlyn," Ian said, a hint of warning in his tone.

"It's okay," Sonny said, laughing. "These happen to be vintage. I get a lot of my clothes from consignment shops and thrift stores. You can find all kinds of old stuff that's become popular again."

"Oh my God! Can we go shopping?" Kimmie asked, bouncing like she had springs in her feet. "Ian has horrible taste and he won't let me buy anything that's in style. It's so—"

"Kimmie, go back to your science project,"

Ian said.

She looked over at him with the annoyed pre-teen eye-roll she'd perfected over the past couple of years. "Fine," she said.

Ian usually called her on the attitude, but right now he just wanted to get her out of the room.

Once she was gone, he wanted to call her back. He hadn't realized just how much of a buffer Kimmie and her insistent chatter had brought. Standing in his kitchen alone with Sonny was an exercise in awkwardness.

"So, the apartment will work for you?" Ian asked.

"Yes. As I mentioned before, I love the size, and the flexible lease agreement is perfect."

And if he counted the steps, Ian was sure it would take less than a hundred of them to get from his bed to hers. The temptation would be so great he wasn't sure how he'd be able to fight it.

"Look, Madison—"

"Sonny," she interrupted. "I usually go by Sonny."

"Yeah, well, when I read the name Sonny in Vanessa's e-mail, I pictured a fat, balding middle-aged guy who'd finally been tossed out of his mom's basement. It may take me a while to get used to calling you Sonny."

She bit her bottom lip, but the smile she was trying to hide still came through her eyes.

"I'd appreciate it if you tried." She hesitated a moment. "Does this mean I get the apartment?"

Ian gave her one curt nod. Then he went around to the other side of the kitchen island. He needed to put some distance between them.

"If you're going to rent the apartment, we need to set some boundaries," he started.

Well-shaped brows peaked over whiskey brown eyes. She crossed her arms and leaned a hip against the counter. "Okay," she said.

Looking toward the dining room where Kimmie was, he lowered his voice and said, "What we did last night will have to be just what it was—that one night."

Her eyebrows shot up. "Wait a minute? Aren't you the same guy who offered to be my new friend who shows me around town and gives me regular orgasms?"

*Damn.* Just hearing her say the word orgasm nearly gave him an orgasm.

"That was before—" Ian took several steps toward her and lowered his voice even more. "That was before I knew there was the possibility of you living above my garage." He released a heavy breath. "Look, I have to think about the kind of example I set for Kimmie. She's only twelve years old."

Sonny hesitated for just a moment before nodding. "I understand where you're coming from. Consider last night forgotten. Do you have a lease for me to sign?"

Ian's head jerked back. Damn, he didn't think she would get over it *that* quickly.

"Not right this minute," he said. "Vanessa is handling all of the paperwork."

"Well, I'd feel better if there was something in writing that I could sign right now, just to make sure you don't rent the room to anyone else," she said. "You can Google 'simple lease agreement' and print something off the Internet, then I can sign the official document once you get it from your real estate agent."

"I'm not going to rent the apartment to anyone else, Sonny."

"You're still offering a month-to-month lease, correct?"

"Yeah. Sure," Ian said.

"Good, because that's a deal breaker for me. I'm not sure how long I'll be in Maplesville."

His head reared back again. "Really? How temporary is this?"

"I'm not sure yet. It all depends on how this new job works out, or if something more suitable comes along. Flexibility is important."

Ian didn't know what to make of the uneasy feeling that settled in his gut at her talking so nonchalantly about moving onto the next town when she'd just arrived in this one.

"We can do the month-to-month thing," he said. "Nothing complicated."

"Great," she said with an overly bright

smile. “So, we’re good?”

Ian stared at her for several long moments before he nodded. “We’re good.”

“Wonderful. I promise you won’t even know I’m here.” She gave him another of those too-cheery-to-be-real smiles before she left out of the kitchen door.

Ian slumped against the counter and cradled his head in his hands.

*Won’t know she’s here?*

As if there was a chance in hell of *that* happening.

# Chapter Three

"Where are you little grater?" Sonny murmured as she searched the huge pullout utensil drawer. "I know you're here somewhere."

The prep station she'd been appointed to at Catering by Kiera wasn't huge but it was well-stocked. She knew there must be a grater somewhere. But she'd been searching for the past five minutes and continued to come up short.

Maybe if she could concentrate on her actual work instead of thinking about her new living situation, she could find what she was looking for.

"It's only temporary," Sonny reminded herself. If she found it too difficult to live in such close proximity to Ian, she could just leave. Simple.

Although finding another apartment that offered a month-to-month lease was probably impossible. Her best bet was to just stay away from Ian altogether.

She had not seen him since Vanessa Chauvin had arrived with the official lease late yesterday afternoon. Other than hearing the rumble of his truck's engine as he backed out of the driveway, she'd managed to avoid all reminders of him.

Okay, so that wasn't *entirely* true. She was constantly reminded of him. There was this humming throughout her entire being all night long, knowing that he was just yards away. She'd fallen asleep thinking about him right next door, having dinner, taking a shower, slipping into bed.

Sonny braced her hands on the stainless steel workstation and searched for her center of control. She had a job to do, and allowing thoughts of Ian's nude body on black silk sheets—because he *had* to sleep in the nude on black silk sheets—would do her no good.

"Concentrate," she admonished with a fierce whisper. It was her first day on the job, and she already had her first big test.

The day began easy enough. Once she arrived, the catering company's owner, Kiera Coleman-Watson, had given her a brief tour of the two thousand square foot corrugated building. After a meeting to discuss dessert ideas for a wedding they would be catering in a couple of weeks, Kiera had left her to become acquainted with the lay of the land.

Sonny had toured through the pantry room and large, walk-in refrigerated room. Then she'd moved just a couple of the baking instruments around—after gaining permission from Kiera, of course—so that they better suited her work style.

She was just settling in when Kiera barged in with an emergency catering job for a law firm downtown. They needed hors d'oeuvres for fifty by noon. Kiera tasked Sonny with coming up with a suitable dessert using whatever she could find in the kitchen because she would not have time to go out and buy supplies.

It had been a mad scramble for Sonny, but also wicked exciting, like something from those Food Network challenge shows, when chefs had to come up with recipes on the fly. Thankfully there was high quality cake flour. As long as she could make a plain yellow cake as a base, Sonny could do just about anything dessert-wise.

She'd baked two large sheet cakes and cut them into small squares. Then she'd dropped several pieces into the plastic shot glasses that she'd spotted during their tour, except for a few cake squares that she'd soaked in a combination of espresso and brandy for tiramisu. Sonny made a mental note to order a few more dessert liquors. Then she could really show what she could do.

That would come later. Right now all she needed was a grater so that she could shave some pieces of the thick bar of dark chocolate that had thankfully also been in the pantry. One thing she'd discovered, when it came to quality, Kiera didn't skimp. Every ingredient she found was top-notch.

"Yes!" Sonny said as she finally located the

grater.

As she made delicate shavings into an empty pie tin, she caught herself smiling. When was the last time *that* had happened while working? Sonny realized this was the difference between doing what you feel you *have* to do as opposed to doing what you *want* to do.

She'd spent the last eight years doing what was expected of her. Her happiness had not been part of the equation, as long as she was holding up the proud White family tradition—being at the very top of her class, earning the highest praise from attending physicians who evaluated her residency program—that's all that mattered.

She could still hear her father's voice.

*There's no such thing as an overachiever.*

Yeah, well, that wasn't her life anymore. Finally, she was doing what *she* wanted to do.

Saying adios to the fake persona she'd perfected over the years was the best thing she could have done. She'd finally revealed the body art she'd hidden from her parents since her first tattoo back in college and had gotten three more just this past year. She'd given up taming her hair with relaxers and let it grow freely. Her unbound 'fro was her crowning glory.

But nothing said *eff you* to her old life more than when she'd dropped out of her residency program to pursue the career she'd always wanted. Her love of baking had been cultivated over those long, lazy summers she'd spent in west Louisiana with her maternal grandmother, Maw Maw Jean, whose cakes and pies were known throughout Cajun country.

Sonny sucked in a deep, shuddering breath.

It was the night before her grandmother's funeral, while Sonny stood in her kitchen baking Maw Maw Jean's famous sweet potato pie for the post-funeral repast, that Sonny decided to quit medicine. Life was too short to spend it doing something she didn't love. Baking was her passion; she owed it to her grandmother to pursue it.

And if she were standing here right now her grandmother would tell Sonny to stop daydreaming and get to work.

Just as she sprinkled the last of the chocolate shavings over the tiramisu, Kiera entered her prep area.

"How's it going in here?" Kiera asked. She stopped short. Her eyes went wide and her mouth dropped open as she perused the dessert cups lined up along the stainless steel table.

"I hope you didn't have these shot glasses set aside for anything in particular," Sonny said. "They were perfect for this dessert. I made individual strawberry shortcakes, lemon curd with blueberry syrup, and tiramisu. You wouldn't happen to have any fresh mint leaves lying around, would you?"

Kiera shook her head as she rounded the table. "These are amazing. I can't believe you were able to come up with this just from what was lying around in the pantry."

"It was a challenge, but it was fun. I think they came out okay."

"You *think*?" Kiera's incredulous smirk wrenched a laugh from her. "I love you for this. Now let's get it over to the law firm."

Kiera's assistant, Macy Bardell, who's electric blue hair had been the first indication to Sonny that Kiera wouldn't have a problem with her own unique style, helped them load everything into the van. Sonny joined Kiera on the delivery so that Macy could prep the food for Kiera's Kickin' Kajun food truck, which would be hitting the streets later tonight.

Sonny climbed into the back of the van so that she could make sure the desserts didn't jostle too much as they drove into downtown Maplesville. The office manager at the law firm was ecstatic when they arrived, thanking Kiera profusely for saving her hide. Their usual caterer, who was an hour away in Covington, had bailed on their standing job to cater the firm's monthly assessment meeting, which was held every third Wednesday of the month. The office manager offered Kiera a contract on the spot to take over all of the law firm's catering duties.

"Did that just happen?" Sonny asked as they made their way back to the van.

"It sure did," Kiera said. "It serves them

right for going with Entertain Us Catering in the first place. I'm the local caterer."

"Is Entertain Us your biggest competitor?"

"They're one of them," Kiera said. "There's another in Slidell that people like to use, even though they're forty-five minutes away. But Entertain Us gives me the biggest run for my money. They have an amazing pastry chef who does competition-caliber cakes. You can thank him for your new job, because he's the main reason I decided to look for a pastry chef. I needed to step up my game if I was going to compete."

"I'll send him a dozen chocolate-covered strawberries as a thank you," Sonny said.

"Oh, I like your sass." Kiera laughed. "Come on, I promised Trey I would deliver lunch for him and his workers at the shop."

As they made their way across town to where Kiera's new husband, Trey Watson's renovation shop was located, Kiera gave Sonny a tour of town.

"Not even five years ago, all of this was sugarcane field," Kiera said, pointing to a line of strip malls and standalone buildings along the main highway. "I don't know what they're building there," she said as they passed a wooded area that was being cleared. "Some speculate that it's a Target. Others say it's a warehouse club."

"Maplesville doesn't seem big enough for a

warehouse club."

"It wasn't big enough for an outlet mall," Kiera said. "But if you build it, they will come." She shrugged as she made a right turn onto a road that was in dire need of repair. "There are a lot of people who are uncomfortable with the massive growth, but it's been good for business. The law firm we just came from is one of several new businesses that have come to Maplesville this past year. There's a huge accounting firm, and further back, around the area where my brother Mason and his wife Jada lives, there's a medical plaza being built in conjunction with the renovations being done at Maplesville General Hospital."

"It looks as if I picked the perfect time to show up," Sonny said.

Kiera peered over at her, an inquisitive lift to her brow. "We didn't really discuss it during your interview, and believe me, it isn't a big deal to me, but do you mind if I ask *why* you chose Maplesville? The town is growing, but it isn't considered a destination for young, single women, especially those with your..." She hesitated. "Your unique style."

Sonny laughed. "I hope you don't have a problem with it."

"Not at all. I love it," Kiera said. "Still, it doesn't scream Maplesville. I just wondered why you picked my hometown."

She knew her new boss must be curious.

Why wouldn't she be? Sonny had been vague about her background during her interview. It was by necessity. It wasn't as if she had a ton of fancy baking credentials to her name. Sonny was certain that it was the chocolate torte she'd made for Kiera on the spot during Monday's interview that won her this job. That and Kiera's willingness to take a chance on her.

Even though she'd dropped out of her residency program over a year ago this was her first official pastry chef job. Most of her business had come from word of mouth, baking cakes, pies and other desserts for friends and family, often having to use their kitchen in order to do so.

That was the one knock against her new apartment; it only had a microwave and cooktop, no oven. But she'd already solved that problem. Because her new boss was the coolest person ever, she'd agreed to let Sonny use the oven at the catering company.

"I moved here for the job," Sonny finally answered. "When I ran across your job posting, it seemed like the perfect fit; somewhere that I could hone my skills and still have time to do some special occasion cakes on the side. You're still okay with me taking side jobs, right?"

"Absolutely," Kiera said. "If someone wants just a cake, it's all on you. I don't want anyone mistaking Catering by Kiera for a bakery. I'm just surprised that you chose a small town instead of a bigger city to get your start."

"The bigger the city, the bigger the competition," Sonny said. "I'll make that move when I think I'm ready."

"All I ask is that you give me at least two weeks notice," Kiera said. "I know we agreed that this is just a trial run, but if you pull off the kind of miracle you did this morning, I may not let you leave. That lemon curd was amazing."

She and Kiera arrived at a midsize corrugated building on the opposite side of Maplesville. A Bluebird school bus sat about fifty yards away. There was a picnic table in front of it and landscaping around the base.

"Someone has taken good care of that old bus," Sonny said.

"Actually, that's Trey's house," Kiera said as she handed Sonny a tray of sandwiches from the back of the van. "We mostly live at my condo downtown, but we spend a few nights a week here."

"You live in a school bus?"

Kiera chuckled. "It's not just any bus. Trey gutted it and remodeled it. The interior rivals a world-class hotel room. That's what he does here at the shop. Actually, he remodeled my food truck. It's how we reconnected after years of being apart."

"That sounds like a story worth hearing," Sonny remarked.

"Oh, it is." Kiera's dreamy sigh said a lot.

"I'll have to tell you about it one of these days. I'll give you a tour of the Bluebird once we've brought the guys their lunch."

They entered the building, which was some sort of mechanics workshop. The moment Kiera's husband came into view, Sonny discovered why her new boss didn't have a problem with her tattoos. Trey's arms were covered with them. The colorful serpent that wound up his forearm and disappeared underneath his snug t-shirt was a fantastic piece of artwork.

Kiera introduced Sonny to Trey as her new pastry chef extraordinaire, and motioned for her to follow them to a small room just to the left of the entrance. The entire room was a cluttered mess. There was just enough room on the table to set out the po'boy sandwiches, cold pasta salad, and chips Kiera had brought for their lunch. Sonny took the left over sheet cake and constructed a three-layer dessert using the lemon curd, berries and whipped cream.

"Damn, Slim, you trying to put us all in a food coma?" Trey said before giving Kiera a quick kiss on the lips. Then he stuck his head out of the door and called, "Lunch's here."

The clang of metal tools being put away rang throughout the building. Two of Trey's workers entered the room and headed straight for the sandwiches. Sonny's hands halted when the third walked through the door.

"Ian?"

"Sonny?" Ian stared at her, complete surprise on his face. "What are you doing here? Is something wrong at the house?" He stopped short. "Wait. How did you know to find me here?"

"I didn't," Sonny said.

"You two know each other?" Kiera asked.

Sonny turned to her. "Ian is my new landlord."

"Seriously?" Kiera laughed. "Talk about a small world."

"You work here?" Sonny asked, even though the answer was obvious. She took in his dusty blue jeans and oil-stained t-shirt. The well-worn cotton clung to his trim, but muscular frame.

She'd found him attractive enough in a suit and tie Monday night, but seeing him like this? She could not handle this much sexy.

She'd spent her life with guys who were brought up in wealthy homes and attended private schools. This raw, gritty thing Ian had going on right now made her belly tingle with all kinds of naughty sensations.

"I work here part-time," Ian answered. "Only when Trey needs an extra set of hands."

"This man knows his way around an engine," Trey said, clamping Ian on the shoulder.

"What are *you* doing here?" Ian asked again.

"Sonny's my new pastry chef," Kiera said, mimicking her husband by clamping her hand over Sonny's shoulder. "This woman knows her way around triple-layer tiramisu." She looked between Sonny and Ian. "I guess Maplesville isn't so big after all, is it?"

"No, it's not," Sonny said.

How was it possible that the one person she'd chosen to have a one-night stand with could be so integrated into her new life? This had to be some big practical joke.

"We should let you guys get to your lunch," Kiera said. "I'm going to show Sonny the Bluebird before we head back. Oh!" Kiera walked up to Trey with a coy grin. "Guess who just picked up a new long-term catering contract with that new law firm in town?"

"That's my Slim," Trey said as he slapped her on the ass. "Make that money, baby."

Kiera sent him a look that was probably supposed to be chastising, but was anything but.

"You're going to pay for that tonight," she said.

He winked. "That's why I did it."

Okay, so maybe she was a little jealous of Kiera and Trey right now. Sonny had never had that kind of sexy, frisky relationship. Probably because Douglas's definition of fun was a lecture on intestinal dissection. She wanted that kind of playfulness in her life.

Would Ian…?

No, she would *not* go there. She was not looking for a relationship, not even a casual one. It was bad enough that they had yet another connection tying them together.

Sonny couldn't even make eye contact with Ian as she followed Kiera out of the room. She could feel his stare on her, burning into her skin.

*Goodness!* Was it really so unreasonable to think that she could have a one-night stand and not encounter him everywhere she turned?

Apparently so.

Ian made an effort to ignore the sensations churning in his stomach as his thumbs drummed on the steering wheel to Wu Tang's "C.R.E.A.M.", but as he turned from Dogwood Lane onto Red Maple Drive, that intoxicating feeling only intensified. Just knowing she would be there made him hard.

"Dammit," he cursed through clenched teeth.

How could he ever think he could survive living just steps away from Sonny? It had only been a couple of days and he was already going insane with the need to have her again.

Ian was still two houses away when he noticed her car parked on the curb a few feet from his mailbox. The passenger side door was open. A firm, denim-covered ass poked out of it.

He slammed on his breaks.

"Christ," he whispered, thankful there was no one behind him.

Causing an accident was the last thing he needed to do right now. He drove past her car and pulled into the driveway. Glancing down at his filthy clothes, Ian cursed himself for not asking to use Trey's shower before coming home.

He shook his head at the ridiculousness of that thought. What was he going to do, shower everyday before coming home? He liked his own shower. Sometimes, he liked to soak in the tub with soft music and candles and shit. He wasn't ashamed to admit that he liked bubble baths every now and then.

But how much better would his bubble baths be if he had some company?

"Don't go there," Ian warned himself.

Sonny backed out of her car holding a cardboard box. She looked over at him and just stood there, staring. Ian realized how much of an idiot he must look like sitting behind the wheel of his pickup in his own driveway.

He climbed out of the truck and walked over to her car, lifting the box from her arms.

"Let me help you," he said. His fingers skimmed over the silken skin of her forearm as she transferred the box, and Ian nearly groaned.

No doubt about it, he would go insane within a week.

"Thank you," she said. "That'll save me a trip."

"How much more do you have?" Ian asked.

"Just a bag and one more box. My old college roommate had been holding some stuff for me at her house in Baton Rouge. We met each other halfway in Hammond this afternoon."

"Why didn't you park in the driveway?" he asked.

"I didn't want to block you out."

"It's your driveway, too, Sonny. You pay rent here, remember?"

"Well, it's a moot point. This is the last of it," she said, gesturing to the car.

Ian hadn't prepared himself for the wave of erotic memories that pummeled him when he peered inside the VW Bug. He would never be able to look at this car without his mind immediately recalling the intense pleasure he'd experienced while crammed into its tiny space. He looked over at Sonny and knew she was thinking about last time they had been in the car together, too. Recalling the things they'd done to each other in the passenger seat.

Ian caught her gaze and held it, refusing to look away.

He deserved just this much, didn't he? To stand here and remember it. Every sound, every smell, every sensual slide of his body inside of hers. If all he'd ever have from that night were the memories, let him have them standing there next to the car where those memories were made. Standing there with the woman who'd provided his body with such bone-deep pleasure.

Sonny was the first to look away, but Ian didn't miss the way her chest expanded with the deep breath she inhaled. Yeah, thinking about that night left him breathless, too.

"We should get these inside," she said.

She grabbed a backpack from the backseat and hoisted it over her shoulder. Then she lifted a plastic milk crate filled with honest-to-goodness vinyl albums from the floor of the passenger side.

Ian motioned for her to go ahead of him up the driveway. He realized his folly once they started up the garage's wooden steps. By the time they reached the landing he was uncomfortably hard behind his zipper, the effects of staring at her perfectly round ass as she climbed the stairs ahead of him.

There would be no hot, soothing bath in his immediate future. Tonight he was taking the coldest shower ever.

As he set the box on the end table where she directed him, Ian looked around the apartment, shocked at how different it looked in just the two days since she'd been there. The normal sea of browns and beiges were now awash in a brilliant display of warm reds, cool blues and bright yellows. Curtains covered the windows that looked out over the backyard and at least a half-dozen African print pillows cluttered the sofa. Equally colorful throw rugs littered the tiled floors.

He walked over to the far wall that was now decorated with three framed posters from the Brooklyn AfroPunk Music Festival. Ian had no idea what AfroPunk was but based on the images on the posters, it suited Sonny.

"It looks…different in here," he said.

"I hope you don't mind. I needed to be comfortable so I added a little bit of me."

"I don't mind." He peered over his shoulder and caught her gaze. "I like little bits of you."

Once again, she was the first to look away. She picked up the carton of albums and moved them over to the small table in the corner where she'd set up a record player. A real one, with a needle and everything.

"It's been a long time since I've seen one of these," Ian said, walking over to the table.

"I collect old albums—another of those things I find in thrift shops. This turntable only looks old school, though. It's equipped with a USB port so that I can transfer the albums to my laptop or even to my phone."

Ian leaned forward, pretending to be interested in the record player when in reality he just wanted to be closer to her. He could smell that hint of spice from whatever scent she wore.

He'd noticed it from the moment she walked up to him at The Corral Monday night, and it had haunted him ever since.

"What is that?" Ian asked.

She looked at him over her shoulder. "What?"

"That scent? *Your* scent."

Her eyes dropped to his lips. "It's, uh, amber. Amber and cloves. It's a mix of essential oils." She eased out of the cove he'd created with his body and the turntable, and walked over to the sofa.

"So," she said, needlessly straightening pillows. "It was a shock to see you at Trey Watson's place today. With that suit you were wearing Monday night, I assumed you were a businessman of some sort. How long have you been working there?"

"I started with him about six months ago, right before Thanksgiving."

She nodded and folded her arms across her chest. "It must be a nice gig," she said. "I mean, it has to be for you to be able to afford a house of this size at your age, right. You can't be more than what? Twenty-five?"

"Twenty-six," he said.

Her brows rose. "Hmm…"

Ian's eyes narrowed as he sensed her discomfort building. She picked up a throw pillow and ran the tasseled edges through her fingers. Then she tossed it back onto the sofa.

"Okay, I was trying to be subtle about this, but you suck at taking hints."

"Sonny, what are you getting at?"

She released a deep sigh. "Just tell me that I won't get kidnapped in the middle of the night by some drug cartel looking for their money," she said.

Ian's eyes widened before he burst out laughing. He clutched his stomach, sucking in several breaths before he could speak. "You think I'm a drug dealer?"

"Well, how do you afford a house like this working as a part-time mechanic?"

"Maybe I'm drowning in debt."

"Are you?"

He laughed again, his shoulders shaking with it. "No, I'm not drowning in debt and I don't sell drugs. In fact, I have never in my life so much as taken a single puff on a cigarette. Do you think I would really put my little sister in that kind of danger?"

"No," she said, looking chagrinned. "But it still begs the question—"

"It's a family home," Ian said, cutting her off. "Technically, it's still my mother's. It's in her name. It'll eventually go to Kimmie."

Her shoulders sank in visible relief. "Thank God. You have no idea how much this has been driving me crazy since you walked into that break room at Trey Watson's shop," she said. "Every crazy scenario you could think of has crossed my mind."

"You may want to lay off the *Law & Order* marathon-watching."

She poked out her tongue. "Shows how much you know. I'm a *NCIS* kind of girl."

"Same thing." Ian moved to where she stood. "As I mentioned at the shop earlier today, I work at Trey's part time. My real job is building scaffolding at the oil refinery over in St. Pierre, about a half hour east of here. I work shiftwork, so when I'm on nights—which I am right now—I'll put in a few hours over at Trey's. I switch back to the day shift tomorrow."

"So, what do you do with Kimmie when you're working the night shift?"

"She stays at her friend, Anesha's. She's just a couple of houses down the street."

Sonny nodded. "Well, now that I'm here, I'll be happy to keep an eye on her. That is, if she's okay with it."

"She's only known you for two days and she already worships the ground you walk on. I think she'd be okay with that. Thanks for offering."

She shrugged. "It's no big deal. Kimmie's a sweetheart."

Moving over to where she stood, Ian perched a hip on the back of the sofa. "It is kinda crazy that we're working for Trey and Kiera, isn't it? They just got married this past New Year's Day."

She nodded.

"With what happened at The Corral on Monday, and you showing up yesterday to rent this place, it almost seems as if the universe is determined to get us together."

"It would seem so," she said.

Her eyes dropped to his mouth again, and Ian's blood began to heat. He licked his lips. Taking another step forward, his voice lowered as he said, "Makes me wonder if it even makes sense to fight it."

Her eyes remained on his lips. "Probably not."

The screech of the school bus's breaks grinding to a halt in front of the house broke the spell between them. Sonny jumped back.

"That must be Kimmie," she said.

*Shit.* Ian released a deep breath. "Yeah."

"Ian!" He could hear Kimmie's glass-cracking scream from outside. "I won first place!"

He gestured to the front windows. "The science fair was today."

"Sounds as if you have a reason to celebrate tonight," Sonny said.

"I was prepared to celebrate even if she came in last place. She worked hard on the project." He hooked a thumb toward the stairs. "I should get down there."

She nodded.

He started down the stairs, but stopped

when she called his name.

"Ian?" He turned to find Sonny at the top of the stairs. "Thanks for helping with the box," she said.

"Anytime," Ian said. "If you need me, you know where to find me."

Then he continued down the stairs, while he was still able to make himself go.

# Chapter Four

Ian glided his forefinger along the computer's touchpad as he scrolled through the two-hundred-plus pre-formatted business card designs under the Automotive and Transportation heading. Was it presumptuous that he was already looking for letterhead even though he had yet to hear back from the bank? Maybe. But as a former Boy Scout, he still adhered to the 'be prepared' motto. He wanted as much in place as possible when it was time to get his bike shop off the ground.

It had been a week since his meeting with Mr. Babineaux. Ian could feel the call coming. Any day now, his phone would ring. It *had* to. He was running out of time.

Ian pulled his phone from his front pocket and read over the text message Vanessa sent late yesterday evening.

*Met with the Miller Family today. They seem close to agreeing on a sale price. Around $400K.*

Vanessa had given him a head's up on the amount she'd advised the family to list the building, so that he wouldn't lowball the amount on his loan application. She'd promised to let him know as soon as the property hit the market. He'd have to have Dale ask her about her favorite wine. She deserved a special treat for the way she'd gone above and beyond to help him secure his dream.

Ian minimized the window with the business card designs and went back to searching for Kimmie's birthday present. He'd bought the Go Pro video camera and the new iPhone she'd been clamoring for since Christmas several weeks ago. Both were in the safe where he kept his important papers and extra cash, tucked in the back of his closet.

Picking out the phone had been the easy part. Finding the perfect phone case had turned into the biggest pain in his ass. He'd automatically gone for a Disney Princess, but he soon realized that as a thirteen-year-old, Kimmie may think she was too old for princesses.

The thought made Ian's stomach twist. He wasn't ready for her to be too old for princesses.

He'd searched through dozens of flower prints, skulls and crossbones, glittery ones covered in fake gemstones. How was he supposed to know what kind of phone cover to buy a thirteen-year-old girl?

*You could ask Sonny.*

No. No he could not ask Sonny. He'd taken an oath to avoid all possible contact with his tenant. Her nearness, even in the most innocuous circumstances, was too much of a temptation.

Why had he insisted on this hands-off thing again?

It had seemed like the adult thing to do at the time. He needed to be a good role model for Kimmie. What kind of example would it set for his sister if she caught him sneaking out of the garage apartment in the middle of the night?

Nevertheless, Ian was getting some serious pressure from his libido to say to hell with being a good role model, especially when he thought about the potential block of uninterrupted hours with Sonny's naked body stretching ahead of him.

But the off chance of Kimmie catching him and Sonny in a compromising position was just one reason sleeping with his boarder again wasn't the wisest idea. If he and Sonny started something up, how awkward would things turn when he had to collect rent from her at the end of the month? Could he really accept money from a woman he was sleeping with?

Yet, if they started sleeping together and he refused to take rent money from her, then it would seem as if he was paying her for services rendered by allowing her to live in the apartment for free.

*Shit*. He was finding complications and nothing had even happened yet.

Hearing the squeak of Kimmie's bedroom door hinge knocked Ian out of his internal debate, and reminded him that he needed to hit those hinges with some WD-40. He quickly minimized the webpage with the iPhone cases. Seconds later he heard Kimmie pounding down the stairs.

She rounded the half wall separating the computer nook from the rest of the family room and hooked an arm around his shoulder.

"Hey, Ian, you know Anesha's older sister, Tamika, right? Well, she's home from college and she brought all kinds of videos from their homecoming party. Can I go over there and watch?"

Ian peered up at her. "Are these college party videos R-rated?"

"Noooo," she answered with the requisite eye roll. "It's a video of the step show between the college sororities and fraternities. Tamika's sorority won first place. I'm going to join a sorority when I go to college, but I'm not sure I'm going to join Tamika's. I like the one with the pink and green colors. I don't know if they are as good in the step shows, but I don't care. So, can I go watch the videos?"

She'd lost him at *college*. Ian was on the verge of hyperventilating whenever he thought about her becoming a teenager in a few weeks. He couldn't handle thoughts of college.

"Be back by six," Ian said.

"*Siiiix*?" She dragged the word out by four syllables. "But Anesha's mom is making lasagna tonight."

"If that's the case, ask her to send me a plate," Ian said. "But I still want you home no later than seven thirty. Mrs. Linh sent an e-mail about tomorrow's social studies test. You need to make sure you're prepared."

That got him another eye roll as she slipped on the high-top Converse she'd brought down from her room.

The moment Kimmie was out of the house, Ian opened up yet another screen he'd minimized earlier, the Google search he'd been doing on birthday parties for thirteen-year-olds. The quest to find a phone case was nothing compared to the nightmare of planning a birthday party.

Kimmie hadn't specifically mentioned that she wanted a party, but ever since one of her classmates had the "party to end all parties" at the skating rink, she'd been dropping subtle hints. Ian pretended he was only casually listening the fifty or so times she'd brought it up.

There was just one problem. He didn't know jack shit about party planning, especially a party for two dozen teens and preteens.

He and Michelle Foster, who'd treated Kimmie like a third daughter ever since Kimmie and Anesha became friends in kindergarten, discussed hosting a sleepover at her house. Ian figured that most parents wouldn't be comfortable with their young daughters attending a slumber party in the house of a single, twenty-six-year-old bachelor. He sure as hell wouldn't allow Kimmie to do so.

He'd assumed the sleepover was the end of it, until Michelle told him that once kids hit a certain age—thirteenish—it was an unwritten rule that they *must* have a coed party so that all of their classmates could attend. Ian balked at the idea at first, but then he remembered back when he was Kimmie's age. Anyone who didn't have a boy/girl party was teased. He didn't want his baby sister getting teased. But *damn*! He absolutely *hated* the thought of this coed thing. Ian knew if he spotted one of those little punks even glancing at Kimmie the wrong way he was going for blood.

In the past Kimmie had been satisfied with cake, ice cream, and having a few of her girlfriends over for Disney movies. But his little sister had grown past the Disney movie stage. It was time for grown up parties. With boys.

"Shit," he whispered.

Ian set his elbows on the computer desk and cradled his head in his hands. He wasn't ready for this. Kimmie had only been nine-years-old when his mother left and he became his sister's legal guardian. Ian hadn't considered what was in store for him just a few years down the road. He hadn't anticipated the cute little girl with a lopsided pigtail—lopsided because he sucked at combing hair—would grow up so quickly.

But she *was* growing up. And he'd soon

have to deal with other things he didn't want to think about, like boys asking her out on dates.

Ian's hands balled into fists just at the thought.

A knock at the kitchen door wrestled his attention away from committing bodily harm on horny pre-teen boys.

He pushed away from the computer, his movements more energetic than they had a right to be as he headed for the kitchen. He already knew who it was. There was only one person who used that kitchen door.

He couldn't help but to be excited at the thought of seeing Sonny, even if it meant torturing himself. It didn't matter that he'd spent the past week trying to avoid her at all costs. Or that he had to constantly fight the urge to creep out to his garage, tiptoe up those steps, and join her in that tiny twin bed.

He really wanted to try out that twin bed with her. With its small size it guaranteed that one of them would have to be on top. He didn't care which one.

Scratch that. He wanted *her* to be on top. For the past week his nightly fantasies centered on her riding him the way she had in her car. He wanted her completely naked this time, her skin slick with sweat, that tattoo he'd peaked at fully exposed.

A shudder tore through his body.

Managing to grab hold of his libido and find

some semblance of control, Ian opened the door to find Sonny burdened by a massive mixing bowl, a rolling pin, and a canvas bag bulging with items he couldn't identify.

"I hate to ask you this," she said, getting a better grip on the bowl. "But I have to get this cake done and there's not enough counter space up there. Can I please use your kitchen?"

"Uh, sure." Ian backed out of the doorway and motioned for her to come inside.

"I was going to just stay late at Kiera's, but the building is undergoing its annual fumigation, so it's off limits. I know this isn't a part of the deal, and I'm willing to pay a little more to rent the space in your kitchen, but I just have to—"

"Sonny, it's cool. This kitchen is mostly used for heating up frozen pizzas and the occasional pot roast. I don't have a problem with you using it."

"Thank you," she said, relief sparkling in her eyes. She deposited the supplies on the kitchen island, then held up a finger. "Be right back," she said, before jogging out of the door. Several minutes later she returned with two round cake pans. "The baby shower I'm baking the cake for isn't until tomorrow, but it's in New Orleans and the mother-to-be is going out there a day early."

"Take as long as you need," Ian said. Then he added, "Just as long as I can get a taste when you're done."

Her head popped up. "A taste of what?"

Their eyes caught and held, and the temperature in the kitchen skyrocketed. Ian backed up against the counter and gripped the edge. He knew he was playing with fire, but he couldn't help it. Just one look at her and all those reasons for not pursuing something with her flew out of his head. He wanted her, dammit.

"Of whatever you're offering," he answered.

Her gaze dropped to his chest, which jutted out because of the way he stood. Her eyes slowly trekked up to his face where they remained for several long moments before she finally tore them away.

She wiped down the counter and then laid a silicon mat over it. "So, where's Kimmie?" she asked as she emptied the contents of the bowl onto the mat.

He decided not to call her on the deflection. After all, they'd both agreed to this hands-off pact. It wasn't Sonny's fault that he was having a harder time sticking to it than she apparently was.

"Kimmie just left for a friend's. She's having dinner there." He paused for a beat, knowing that he shouldn't continue, but unable to stop himself. "She won't be back until after seven tonight."

There was no need to point out that they would be alone in the house for hours, was there? That they were free to reenact that first encounter they had in the parking lot of The Corral in every single room if they chose to do so? It had to be as obvious to her as it was to him, right?

*You said "hands-off."*

And he hadn't given Sonny any indication that he wanted them to reconsider the arrangement they'd settled on. Maybe he *did* have to explicitly spell it out.

"We already decided it wouldn't be a good idea," Sonny said, as if she'd been reading his mind the entire time.

Ian wondered if she realized just how much that dagger she'd just stabbed straight to his heart pained him?

She stopped rolling out the fondant icing and looked up at him. "It would just complicate things, and neither of us need complications. Right?" She added, as if she wasn't sure. He sure as hell had started to question that decision they'd made last week.

Ian wanted to argue that *technically* it wouldn't be a complication since Kimmie wasn't there, and thus *technically*, wouldn't be influenced one way or another by any wild monkey sex they may have within the next hour. But that was his other head talking, and he wouldn't allow himself to be controlled by that part of his anatomy.

"You're right," Ian said. He ran a palm

along the back of his head, trying to rub some sense into what had become a one-track brain. "It kills me that you're right, but…damn…you are."

Ian pushed away from the counter and gestured to her cake. "I'll leave you to your baking."

Their eyes connected again, and the mixture of wanting and regret staring back at him nearly did him in.

"Thanks again for letting me use the kitchen," she said.

He lifted his shoulders in a hapless shrug. "Like I said, anything you need, all you have to do is ask."

Sonny slipped the muffin tin into the oven, then returned to the cake she'd been working on. With painstaking gentleness she carefully lifted the sheet of cotton candy pink fondant from the mat and draped it over the buttercream-frosted four-layer round cake. She gently glided the smoothing tool over the fondant, pressing away excess wrinkles. Spinning the cake around on the base, she did the same with the sides, until it looked flawless.

Then she paused for a moment to take a deep breath.

She'd had to do that off and on for the past

twenty minutes, because just thinking about Ian in the next room, along with this big empty house they currently had to themselves, literally made her breathless.

Why did this have to be so difficult?

Those complications they'd discussed seemed so insignificant now. So what if it would make things awkward between them? If ever someone had proven that they were worth a little awkwardness, it was Ian. Their encounter in her car was never far from her mind, and when he was sitting just a few yards away from her with a bed or a sofa or, hell, even the floor at their disposal?

Sonny shut her eyes and searched for her center of control.

She had a job to do. This was only the second cake job she'd scored since she arrived in Maplesville, but it was a start. She needed it to be as close to perfect as she could make it.

She was snipping away the excess fondant hanging from the bottom of the cake when she heard, "Hey, Sonny, can I bother you for a minute?"

She looked up to find Ian just inside the kitchen entryway, his shoulder leaning against the trim. She was *not* going to focus on the way his dark blue t-shirt stretched across his chest. She refused to even let her mind go there.

Of course, her mind had an agenda of its own, namely soaking in as much eye-candy as possible.

"Sure, what do you need?" she asked.

He huffed out an awkward laugh. "That's a loaded question."

"Ian—"

He held both hands up. "I know, I know. We're avoiding complications. This is for something different," he said. "I need some party planning advice. Kimmie's birthday is in a few weeks and I want to throw her a surprise party."

Totally not what she was expecting. Her heart may have melted just a bit.

"That's so sweet."

The way he shifted from one foot to the other, showing clear discomfort at her praise, melted Sonny's heart the rest of the way.

"It's nothing big," Ian said. "I'm planning to just throw her something here at the house. She's also going to have a slumber party at her friend's, but I was warned that it would be a mistake not to have a party where boys were allowed."

"How old will she be?"

"Thirteen."

"Thirteen?" Sonny nodded vehemently. "You *must* have a boy/girl party if she's turning thirteen. And you can forget about it being 'nothing big.' She's becoming a teenager. You have to give her a party that's fit to commemorate such an exciting event."

His dour expression wrenched a laugh out of her.

"Why do you look as if you're ready to lose your breakfast?" Sonny asked.

"Have you ever planned a party for a thirteen-year-old before?"

"No."

"Then you wouldn't understand."

She managed to swallow her laugh. "No more frowning," she said. "This is going to be fun. And it's perfect timing. I just slipped my third layer in the oven and my safety pins need to harden a bit more."

Pushing the tray of pink, yellow and white safety pins she'd fashioned out of gumpaste to the side, Sonny wiped her hands on the front of her apron as she rounded the kitchen island. Then she took the apron off and folded it over the back of a kitchen stool.

When she looked over at Ian, he was staring at her with an odd expression.

"What?" Sonny asked.

He nodded toward her hands. "I just noticed all your rings are gone. Your hands look strange without them."

She splayed her fingers. "Yeah, well they're not very conducive to baking."

"It's a shame. Those rings are a part of what makes you…well…you. They're a part of your style."

Sonny reached in the front pocket of her

jeans and came out with a fist full of rings. “They’re never too far.” She smiled as she slipped the rings on her fingers.

“That’s better.” Ian’s answering grin had just enough of that flirtatious sexiness she’d already come to anticipate. And those eyes. Goodness, but she loved the way his eyes crinkled at the corners when he grinned.

She wondered just how long Kimmie would be at her friends’.

*Oh, no you don’t!*

“So, what party plans have you made so far?” Sonny asked, shoving away those tempting thoughts.

“None,” Ian answered.

Sonny’s mouth dropped open. “Her birthday is just weeks away and you haven’t even started planning yet?”

He hunched his shoulders. “That’s why I came to you for help. I’m desperate.”

“Oh, Ian, Ian, Ian. You have much to learn. Come on.”

She grabbed him by the hand and tugged him toward the computer station. Once he was seated, Sonny stood behind him, clamped her hands on his shoulders, and crouched forward, peering at the screen.

She felt Ian stiffen. He looked up at her over his shoulder. “If you want to avoid complications you may want to stop touching me,” he said.

Sonny jerked her hands away as if his skin was on fire. "Sorry," she said.

"It's for the best. That's what we decided, right?"

"Right," she said. She swallowed hard.

Ian's fist clenched. He released a deep breath before speaking, "It's a lot harder than you thought it would be, isn't it?"

"Yes," Sonny admitted. "But I still think it's the smart decision. For both of us."

He looked up at her over his shoulder. "You sound so sure about that."

"I am, Ian. Despite what happened last Monday, I don't make a habit of sleeping with someone I'm not in a relationship with, and starting a relationship is not a part of my plans right now. You were supposed to be that one night."

"Your little indiscretion," he said, his smile lacking the playfulness it usually exhibited.

"More like an indulgence." She said. "The fact is, I spent so much of my life doing what others wanted me to do, that yielding to my own wishes doesn't come easy for me. I'm still learning how to put my wants first. And when I saw you, I wanted you. Allowing myself to do what we did last Monday night was huge. But taking it any further just wouldn't..." She shook her head. "It's just not a good idea."

Sonny didn't want any strings tying her to this place when it was time for her to leave, and something told her that getting romantically involved with Ian would tie her in one huge knot.

"Are we on the same page?" Sonny asked, her voice hopeful.

His smile was reluctant, but at least he was smiling. "Yeah," Ian said. "Did I ever thank you for letting me be your indulgence?"

She laughed. "Renting me the apartment is thanks enough. Now, back to party planning." She turned him back toward the computer screen. "What does Kimmie enjoy the most?"

"Movies," Ian said. "No question about it. From old black and white flicks, to Disney movies, to action films and even Bollywood, which I didn't even know was a thing until she made me sit and watch them with her. She wants to be a director when she grows up."

"No kidding," Sonny said, impressed. "Good for her. Hollywood needs more black directors behind the camera. A black woman director is even better." She clapped her hands together. "Okay, so this will be easier than I thought. It goes without saying that her party should have a movie theme."

"That's what I thought at first, but don't you think the kids may get bored with just watching movies? I wanted to do something a little more exciting."

"I didn't say they would sit around and watch movies the entire time. We'll have the movies playing in the background, but that will only be a small part of it."

"As long as it's better than a party at the skating rink."

"Why?" Sonny asked, her brow creasing with confusion.

"One of Kimmie's friends held her birthday party at the skating rink not too long ago. Apparently, Jerica is now the envy of every girl in school."

"Good. We have a goal. Beat the skating rink party." Sonny snapped her fingers. "Oh, I know! You should rent one of those inflatable projector screens. Have you seen them?"

Ian shook his head.

"It would be perfect. You can set it up in the backyard and make it look like a movie drive-in. How many kids are you expecting?"

"Uh, about twenty maybe?"

"Twenty teens? You could probably get by with four trucks, although five would be even better."

"Five trucks for what?" Ian asked, his face the textbook definition of overwhelmed.

"For Kimmie's Movie Drive-In Birthday Bash," Sonny said. She pushed his rolling chair to the side and started tapping away on the keyboard.

"I'll share with you the first tip when it comes to party planning. You can find whatever you need on Pinterest." She pointed at the screen. "These little cars made out of cardboard boxes are adorable, but you can't have that for a thirteen-year-old's party. A better alternative is to get four or five pick-up trucks, put some pillows and blankets in the truck bed, and let them watch the movies from there. Just like an old fashioned drive-in."

Ian scowled. "I don't know if I like the idea of a boy/girl party that includes pillows, blankets and beds of any kind. Even truck beds."

"The overprotective thing is cute, but you're interfering with my party planning." She scrolled through the mishmash of photos. "We can set up a concession stand with popcorn, and nachos, and boxes of movie theater candies. And I have a killer idea for her birthday cake."

She typed in *movie themed birthday cake* and brought up a picture of a four-tiered cake that looked like old-fashioned film reels stacked one on top of the other. The very top layer was in the shape of a red and white box of popcorn, with a director's clapboard leaning against it.

"You can make this?" Ian asked with a hint of disbelief.

"I made this one," Sonny said. She couldn't disguise the pride in her voice even if she tried. Which she didn't. That cake was one of her best creations yet.

"You *made* this?" Ian swirled his chair around to face her. "No way."

"Yes way," she said. She clicked on the

picture, which took her to the blog post of the local actress who'd hired her for the job a couple of months ago when she was bunking at Karen's. "The cake was for a viewing party for a woman who was an extra in a show being filmed just outside of Baton Rouge."

"Wow," Ian said. "That's a pretty awesome cake."

"*Pretty* awesome? That cake kicks ass."

He held his hands up, a deep chuckle shaking his shoulders. "Okay, you're right. The cake totally kicks ass. It can stand on its own. No need for anything else at the party."

"Oh, no you don't," Sonny said. She turned the computer screen so they both could see it. "We're going to throw Kimmie a kickass party to go along with her kickass cake. By the time her friends leave, they won't remember that dinky skating rink party."

"Sounds like a plan." He caught her by the forearm. Sonny looked down to where his hand covered her, then back up to his face. "Thanks," Ian said. "I didn't know the first place to start when it came to this party. I was so afraid I'd mess it up and ruin everything for Kimmie."

"There's no need to thank me, Ian. I'm happy to help. Kimmie is a sweetheart. She deserves the kind of party that she'll remember forever."

"You mean one that she'll remember for the right reasons, and not because her older brother embarrassed her."

Sonny grinned. "You will *always* embarrass her. You embarrass her by merely existing." She patted his arm. "But don't take that stank attitude she throws at you personally. Most of the time she doesn't mean it. I can remember what it was like to be a thirteen-year-old girl. It's both horrifying and exhilarating. I was such an awkward duck."

"No way."

"Yes." She nodded. "I was taller than all of my friends. I wore braces. And my parents could not care less about keeping up with the latest fashions, so my clothes were lame."

"You sound like Kimmie."

"She's at that age where this stuff is her entire world. Being a teenage girl isn't always easy."

"Yeah, well imagine what it's like trying to *raise* one," Ian said. He massaged his temples. "I could have used you when she got her first period. It was a freaking nightmare. I cried more than Kimmie did."

She stared at him for a moment before she burst out laughing. At the same time the rest of Sonny's heart melted at the sincerity in his voice. It was hard enough fighting her attraction to him. When he reminded her just how sweet he was with all that he did for his little sister, it was too much.

"At least Kimmie seems to appreciate how

much you spoil her."

The affront on his face was laughable. "I don't spoil her."

"Yes, Ian, you do. I've only been around you two for a week and I can see that. But I've also witnessed her hauling laundry from the clothes dryer in the garage and doing homework as soon as she comes home from school, so you balance it out."

"I still don't think I spoil her," he said.

His cell phone rang. He nearly toppled out of the chair as he reached for it over by the printer.

"That has to be the bank," he said. He answered and started slowly pacing between the kitchen and the living room.

Sonny pretended not to listen to his side of the conversation as she scrolled through the endless pictures on Pinterest, but she could tell by his weighty pauses that whatever was being relayed on the other end of the phone wasn't what he wanted to hear.

She heard a stern, "Not the house. That's not up for debate."

Another pause. Ian stopped pacing.

"The house isn't even in my name," he said. "I can't offer it up, and I wouldn't do it anyway. The house cannot be a part of the equation."

Then she heard, "I'll get back to you by the end of the day," before Ian released a sigh and shoved the phone in his front pocket.

Sonny looked over and gestured at the phone. "Was that something you want to talk about, or are you good?"

He shook his head. "Nah, I'm good. Possibly," he tacked on. He ran a hand down the back of his head. "Shit."

Okay, so he definitely was not good. Something was up. Something that was *not* her concern. He'd asked her to help plan his little sister's party, not become involved in his life.

But it was hard not to become involved, given their living arrangement. She'd found herself in Ian's kitchen or the family room or Kimmie's bedroom on several occasions over the past week. The younger girl had a serious case of hero worship, but Sonny didn't mind. Despite Ian spoiling her like crazy, Kimmie was sweet and respectful. And even though she talked more than just about anyone Sonny had ever met, it was just another thing that she found endearing about her.

As for Kimmie's older brother…

Well, the list of things she found endearing about him took on an entirely different tone.

But none of that mattered right now. Right now, Sonny was more concerned about the tension lines bracketing Ian's mouth. She wasn't sure what was going on, or if she would be able to provide any insight, but it didn't feel right to sit here and watch him suffer alone.

"Tell me," Sonny said. "Maybe talking it out

will help."

He stared at her for a moment before releasing another of those bone-deep breaths and coming back over to the computer nook. He didn't sit in the chair he'd vacated a few minutes ago, choosing instead to perch his butt against the desk. He crossed his legs at the ankle and folded his arms over his chest.

"I want to start my own bike shop," he began. "It's been a dream of mine for a long time—a dream I shared with my dad. But I need a loan from the bank in order to make it happen. That was the loan officer. He said they would be more 'comfortable' if I had something else to put up for collateral."

"Something like this house." She'd gleaned that much from his side of the phone conversation.

"Yes, but that's not going to happen. The house isn't mine."

He'd told her the house was in his mother's name.

"I'm not sure what all the legalities are, but I'm sure there's a way to get the house put in your name if that's what's stopping you. It may take some time, but—"

"All it would take is a call to my mom asking her to sign the house over to me," Ian said.

Sonny stopped short. "Wait, your mom is alive?"

He nodded.

That's not what she was expecting. She hadn't wanted to pry, but had wondered all week about his parents. Sonny had assumed they were both dead. It seemed the only logical reason for why someone as young as Ian was raising his little sister.

"My mom's living somewhere in Paris," Ian said. "Or maybe she's moved to the south of France. I think she mentioned something like that the last time I spoke to her. And before you ask, the reason I never bothered to have the house put in my name is because I'm planning to have my mom sign it over to Kimmie when she turns eighteen. It's the only way to make sure her future is secure."

"But maybe you can—"

"There are no 'but maybes' when it comes to this." Ian shook his head. "I would never use this house as collateral for a loan. I'll just have to figure out something else."

Sonny's gaze searched his face. She didn't want to pry, but the question pounding in her brain demanded an answer.

"I hope you don't mind my asking, but how did you end up raising Kimmie?"

He shrugged. "My mom decided she could no longer do it."

Sonny couldn't tell if he really was as indifferent about it as he appeared, or if the nonchalance was an act he'd perfected just to make it seem that way.

"How long ago did she leave the States?" Sonny asked.

He tilted his head to the side and scrunched his forehead. "Kimmie had just turned nine, so about four years ago."

Which meant Ian had just turned twenty-two. What kind of person left her twenty-two-year-old son to raise her nine-year-old daughter?

"And your dad?"

"He died in an accident at work when I was seventeen. At the same oil refinery where I work," he said.

She just barely held in her gasp. "I'm so sorry," Sonny said. The words seemed so inadequate. "I can't imagine how hard that must have been for you, especially at that age."

"It was hard for all of us," he said. "Especially my mom. That's why I wasn't all that surprised when she decided she could no longer live here. She…she needed to get away.

"The fifth year anniversary of my dad's accident did something to her. I think she had a break with reality, or a midlife crisis or something. Do women have those?" He huffed out a humorless laugh and shook his head. "Anyway, it's better for Kimmie that she's not around. She'd probably have her going from one school to the other, dragging her around the country, or worse she'd be miserable having to live here in Maplesville with those memories and would blame Kimmie for it. I couldn't allow that to happen. My dad would have wanted me to take care of both my mom and Kimmie, and allowing my mom to leave was the best thing I could have done for both of them."

Although he spoke as if his mother's leaving was no big deal, Sonny could hear the resentment in his voice.

"In a way, my dad is still taking care of her. It's the worker's comp settlement from his accident that made it possible for my mom to move to France. Dad would have wanted it that way. The two of them used to talk about going there when he was alive."

"But what about you and Kimmie? The two of you need to be taken care of, as well. Did you get anything from the accident?"

He nodded. "Kimmie will continue to receive weekly death benefits from his worker's comp until she's twenty-two, the same as I did. There's also money from an insurance settlement with the contractor who was in charge of the project, but because Kimmie and I were minors when the accident happened, the money was put into individual trusts. I won't have access to mine for another few years. Something about saving on the estate tax by holding it until I'm thirty instead of releasing the money now."

"It may be worth it to take the early withdrawal penalty," she said.

"I considered that, but it still wouldn't be

enough to buy the building. That's what the loan is for," he explained. "The perfect spot for my bike shop—the place I've had my eye on for years—is about to go on the market. Vanessa is the real estate agent handling the sale. She's going to be flooded with buyers as soon as she lists it, so I want to be able to make an offer at or even above the asking price the morning it goes up for sale.

"The night we met? I was celebrating at The Corral because my meeting to get pre-approval for the loan went so well. I didn't take into account that the bank may be reluctant to approve a single, 26-year-old with limited credit history for $400,000."

Sonny grimaced. "I hate to say it, but that would be a tough sale for any loan officer. Especially the limited credit history."

Ian held his hand out and hunched his shoulders. "It never crossed my mind that it could be a problem. I make good money at my job, the house is paid for, and between my dad's social security and the money my mom sends for Kimmie every month, all the rest of the bills are covered. I have no reason to buy anything on credit. I thought I was being responsible by not running up a ton of credit card bills. Instead, it's coming back to bite me in the ass."

"Are you sure there's nothing else you can do?" Sonny asked. "Nowhere else you can find the money?"

He shook his head. "I'll think of something. Let's get back to party planning." He looked over at the door. "Actually, I should probably try to get the rest of Kimmie's birthday presents ordered before she gets back."

"What's her present?"

"The iPhone she's been wanting forever," he answered. "At least that's one of them. I'm also surprising her with this television and film summer camp in New York that she's wanted to go to. Most of your rent money is going into a fund to cover her room and board and spending money while she's out there."

"And you don't think you spoil her?" she asked with a laugh.

"Hey, you're the one who said turning thirteen is this monumental event for a girl. It deserves a nice gift, doesn't it?"

"There's a huge difference between a nice gift and what you're doing, but I understand it better now that you've explained the situation with your mom."

His brow furrowed. "What do you mean?"

Sonny debated whether or not she should say anything else, but Ian's focused expression demanded she elaborate.

"Don't take this as me trying to psychoanalyze the situation or anything, but all the gifts seem like a way to make up for Kimmie having to grow up without her mom and dad."

"That's not—" he started, but then he

stopped. "Shit," Ian whispered. "Who knows. Maybe I do spoil her because of the way my mom left."

"At least you're not turning her into a brat. As I said before, she seems to appreciate everything you do for her."

"Yeah, well, maybe if I'm able to pull off this surprise party I can qualify for the Best Big Brother in the Entire World award.

"Actually, I think you've already earned that."

A grin stole across his lips. "Close, but I'm not there yet."

"Says who? Seriously, Ian, how many twenty-two-year-old males do you know who would step in to raise their nine-year-old sister?"

"I did what I had to do. If I hadn't she would have been shipped to my great aunt Dolores in Jackson, Mississippi. She smells like stale bread and peppermint. I couldn't do that to Kimmie."

Sonny laughed. She had to stop herself from wrapping her arms around him and burying her face against his neck. The fact that he evoked that kind of response in her rocked Sonny to her core.

Ian was the total opposite of the type of guy she'd dated in the past. If her ex had been in his position, Sonny had no doubt that Douglas would have gladly shipped his little sister to his peppermint-scented aunt. She couldn't imagine him being considerate enough to even remember a child's birthday, let alone want to throw said child a surprise party.

She looked over at Ian and wondered what she'd ever seen in her ex. She shuddered to think of what her life would be like right now if she hadn't put her foot down and called off that engagement.

Miserable. That's what her life would be like right now. One long miserable day after another.

But look at her now. On top of her fabulous new job with Kiera, she'd already baked two cakes as a part of her side business. Eventually, if she played her cards right, her cake designing skills would become her main business.

If only she could forget about those pesky *complications* that were preventing her and Ian from becoming anything more, her life would be damn near perfect.

Sonny rounded the chair and walked up to him. Without thinking, she cradled his cheek in her palm and said, "Don't worry yourself over it. Good things come to good people, and as far as I can tell, you are very good people, Ian Landry."

His gaze grabbed hold of hers as his hand came up to cover the one she'd placed on his cheek.

"If that were true we would be doing more than just standing here," he said. He leaned forward, until his lips were only a hairsbreadth from hers, and said, "We would be doing this."

The moment those ridiculously soft lips

touched hers Sonny was catapulted to an entirely new world. A world where only she and Ian existed. A world where they could explore each other with abandon. Tasting each other, consuming each other.

His kiss was tentative at first, but when she licked at the seam of his lips, it exploded into a haze of teeth and tongue. His taste drove her wild, a deep, spicy mixture unlike anything she'd ever experienced before. With a boldness that was intoxicating, Ian's tongue dove into her mouth, inhaling her as his hands traveled up and down her back.

It was as if an inferno erupted inside of her. Sonny wrapped her arms around him, pulling her body flush against his. She could feel him hardening against her stomach. The physical evidence of his desire grew stronger by the second, triggering sensations that turned her insides to liquid.

Something in the back of Sonny's mind told her she needed to put an end to this right this second, instead, she said in a desperate whisper against Ian's lips, "If you wrap my legs around your waist and carry me up the stairs, I won't complain."

"You promise?" Ian replied.

She nodded. "Please. Carry me up the stairs."

Just then the oven timer buzzed loud enough to wake the dead. She and Ian both jumped, breaking apart.

"What the hell is that?" Ian asked.

"Your oven timer," Sonny answered with a sigh.

"Shit." He ran a hand down his face. "That damn near gave me a heart attack."

"Which one?"

He looked up at her and grinned. "Take a guess."

Sonny's eyes fell onto his slightly red lips and she held in a sigh. Goodness, could she want him more than she already did? She doubted it, yet she was grateful for the interruption. Giving in to temptation would only lead to her doing something she would regret.

Or would she?

*Of course you would,* she argued with her conscience. Later that afternoon, after she had time to clear her head, she would try to remember just what those regrets were. For the life of her, she couldn't recall a single one right now.

Sonny pointed over her shoulder. "My cake is ready," she said.

Ian nodded. "You should probably get back to work." He pointed to the clock shaped like the Eiffel Tower, something Sonny now suspected was a remnant of when his mother had lived here. "I'm back on nights, so I should take a nap before my shift anyway," he said.

He started up the stairs.

"I'll try to keep it down in the kitchen," Sonny called after him.

Ian glanced over his shoulder. "Probably doesn't matter. I doubt I'll get much sleep."

# Chapter Five

Ian heard the thump of Madison's car door slam and had to practically order his heartbeat to remain steady. It truly was the sweetest torture in the world, living so close to her, imagining how things would be if they gave in to the powerful chemistry that pulsed between them. His current favorite nighttime fantasy was thinking about what would have happened if the oven timer had not gone off the other day and interrupted what would have undoubtedly led to some of the best sex of his life.

*Dammit.*

He knew it would have been spectacular.

What stunned him the most in these last two weeks was how well they got along when they were not naked in the front seat of her car, despite the fact that they were complete opposites. She had this natural, carefree vibe about her, while his main focus was on work. But in those little snippets of time when he wasn't at the refinery, or at Trey's, or here in the garage working on a bike, he loved spending whatever time he could with Sonny.

He hoped like hell that she had a cake to bake today. He'd become accustomed to hanging out in his kitchen, watching with no small amount of awe as she turned flour, water and sugar into a work of art. The only thing Ian didn't like about it was how their conversations eventually turned into her talking about moving to a bigger city and opening up her own boutique cake business. She'd barely arrived in Maplesville and she was already thinking about the next city she would move to.

He couldn't help but think about what might happen at the end of the month. Would she choose to stay, or would she pack up those vinyl albums and colorful throw pillows and say adios to this town? A rancid taste flooded his mouth at the thought.

The side door opened and Sonny stepped through. Her huge afro was as wild as ever. She wore tight jeans, a suede vest with long fringe that started just under her breast and fell nearly to the tattoo at her waist, and huge amber-colored sunglasses covering half her face. The smile that graced her lips at the sight of him was everything Ian needed in life right now.

"Hi," she greeted.

"Hey," Ian said. He slung the oil-smudged rag he'd used to clean the carburetor onto his worktable and wiped his fingers on a clean one. Then, unsure what to do with his hands, he picked up the torque wrench and started in on the stubborn lug nut he'd been trying to remove. "Done already at Kiera's?" he asked.

She nodded and pulled the glasses from her

eyes, hooking them between her breasts. Of course, now all he could do was think about her breasts.

"We spent much of today prepping for some church fair happening this weekend."

"St. Michael's," Ian said. "It's that huge Catholic church over on Wisteria Boulevard. Their spring festival is legendary around here."

"That's what Kiera told me. We're bringing the food truck out there." She gestured to the Yamaha he'd rescued from a salvage yard north of Denham Springs a few months ago. "So, are those the type of bikes you'll be selling in your shop?"

Ian's attention remained on the delicate shadows created by her cleavage.

Sonny clapped her hands together. "Hello, earth to Ian."

"What?" he asked, shaking his head.

"The motorcycle? Is it the kind you plan to sell in your new bike shop?"

Ian lifted a shoulder. "Sure. Along with whatever else I can get my hands on."

He gave the torque wrench a yank and heard a pop, followed by a sharp pain. "Shit," Ian cursed, holding his finger against his chest.

Sonny was at his side in an instant. "What happened?" She tugged his hand away from his chest. "Let me see it."

"I think…think I broke it," Ian said, his teeth clenched.

"It's not broken, just dislocated," Sonny said. She caught the tip of his injured finger and popped it back into place. "How does that feel?" she asked.

"Still hurts like a bitch." Ian tried to wiggle his finger.

"No, don't move it just yet. You need to put some ice on it and take a couple of pain relievers. Give me a sec."

She went upstairs to her apartment and just a few minutes later returned with a Ziploc bag filled with crushed ice, a bottle of water and two pills. She handed him the pills and uncapped the water bottle before placing it in his uninjured hand.

"Keep the ice on it for at least ten minutes. It'll numb the pain and prevent swelling. It should already feel a little better now that the joint is back in place."

"It does," Ian said. "How did you do that? My finger," he said. "Where did you learn what to do?"

She looked up at him. "In, um, in medical school," she said.

Ian's head jerked back. "Wait. You went to medical school?"

She nodded. "I got through one year of residency, but things didn't work out. So." She hunched her shoulder.

"So you decided to bake cakes? That's a pretty big change."

"Yes, but I'm *much* happier baking cakes than I ever was in the ER," she said. She glanced up at him before continuing. "I wasn't in medical school because I wanted to be a doctor. I was there because everyone else thought I should become a doctor. It was never discussed. I was never even asked if it's what I wanted. It just..." She hunched her shoulders. "Happened."

"All those years of school don't just happen."

"They do when you're Carter White's daughter." Her words, though spoken lightly, held a trace of bitterness. "My dad's a doctor. He wanted me to follow in his footsteps."

"What about your mom?"

"She's the executive director of a nonprofit in Houston."

Ian let out a low whistle. "Sounds like the bar is set pretty high in the White household, huh?"

"You have no idea." She huffed out a brief, humorless laugh. "Maybe I should call my dad and tell him all my medical training was finally put to use." She nudged her chin toward his finger. "How is it feeling?"

"A hell of a lot better than it did ten minutes ago."

"That's probably because it's numb from the ice. It's going to be sore for a while."

"Well, I guess it's a good thing I've got you living right next door." He started to speak again, then stopped.

"What?" Sonny asked.

"I was going to make a joke about the two of us playing doctor, but it sounded lame even to me."

"Thanks for sparing me," Sonny said with a laugh. She ambled over to the bike and ran her finger along the reddish-orange engine cover. "I've never ridden one of these before."

"To be honest, I haven't been out for a ride in a couple of months," Ian admitted.

She whipped around to face him, her forehead creasing with confusion. "You rebuild bikes but you don't ride them?"

"I do, usually. I just haven't had much time since I started working for Trey." He looked at her. "Do you want to?"

"What? Ride your motorcycle?"

Actually, if she were going to ride something of his, the motorcycle would be his second choice.

"I don't know," Sonny said, staring at the bike with a cautious dip to her brow, but Ian thought he sensed a bit of excitement lurking behind her gaze. She wanted to take a ride.

"Come on," Ian said. "You know you want to."

"I've seen the results of enough motorcycle accidents to know better than to get on one, especially with someone nursing an injured finger at the helm."

"My finger is feeling better already. Come on, Sonny. I promise it'll be safe," Ian said. "Besides, I owe you a tour of Maplesville. You've been here two weeks and still only know this house and Kiera's catering company."

"And The Corral," she said.

She looked up at him, her eyes wide, as if she let the words slip without thinking.

"Yeah," Ian said after a deep breath. "We can't forget about The Corral."

There was that electricity again, humming between them like a live wire. God, he wanted this woman. He wanted her so damn much.

"You promise to be safe?" she asked him. "No showing off with crazy motorcycle tricks?"

"Never," Ian said. "I've got Kimmie to take care of, remember? I'd never do something reckless on the bike. It'll just be a nice stroll around Maplesville." He paused for a beat before he said, "Maybe I can entice you to stay a bit longer."

There was only a brief flash of indecision in her eyes before she said, "Okay. I'll go for a ride on your bike."

*Yes!* He knew he'd get her to cave sooner or later.

"Just give me a minute to clean up."

She eyed him up and down. "I don't know. I kinda like you dirty."

Ian sucked in a swift breath and released it with a moan. "I had no idea you were so damn wicked."

She bit her lip between her teeth, but couldn't hold in her laugh.

He took the quickest shower of his life, and threw on a pair of old jeans and a t-shirt he'd grabbed from the laundry still waiting to be folded and put away. He was back in the garage in less than ten minutes.

Sonny was sitting atop his worktable, her sexy legs crossed at the ankle.

"You ready?" Ian asked.

She scooted off the table. "Which bike?"

He pointed to the black and gold Honda. He'd been working on it for weeks now. This would be the perfect opportunity to test it out.

"So, where do you want to go?" he asked her.

"You're the one giving me the tour," she said, "Take me wherever you think I'd have the most fun."

Ian's voice took on a husky note. "If that's the case we don't have to get on the bike at all."

"Fully clothed," she said.

He snorted as he unhooked a helmet from a peg on the garage's wall and held it out to her. "I thought out of the two of us *you* were supposed to be the carefree risk-taker?"

"Nice try." She turned the helmet around in her hands. "It'll be a miracle if I can get all my hair inside that thing," Sonny said.

Ian raised the garage door and walked the

Honda out, then lowered the door behind them. He climbed on the machine, which if he were being honest, could use a washing before going out about town, and kicked the kickstand back.

He tipped his head. "Climb on," he said to Sonny.

"Just a minute," she said. She'd put her sunglasses back on, so she tipped her head down slightly. "I just have to look at you for a minute on that thing." She released a slow breath. "Nice."

He took the opportunity to study her as well. She'd managed to fit her 'fro inside the helmet, despite her previous doubts. While he was showering she'd changed into heeled boots that came just up to her calves. The sight of that sleek leather hugging her legs had him adjusting his position on the bike.

When she climbed on behind him and wrapped her arms around his waist, it only added to the situation behind his fly. He'd had more hard-ons in the two weeks since Sonny had been here than in the past three months combined.

"So, where're you taking me?" she asked.

Ian started up the bike and revved the engine. "You'll find out when we get there."

He pulled out of the driveway and headed for downtown. Ian gave her the back lot tour of Maplesville, traveling to the older part of town that hadn't been as affected by all the new growth taking place along the main highway. They swung by Hannah's Ice Cream Shoppe—the old-fashioned ice cream parlor was a must-see—and shared a banana split that was big enough to feed four. Watching Sonny slip spoonful after spoonful of rich ice cream in her mouth aroused him way more than it should have. Of course, just watching her breathe aroused him.

Once they were done with their ice cream they continued toward the center of town.

He hadn't planned on it, but in just a few minutes Ian found himself parking the bike on the brick sidewalk in front of the old Miller Pharmacy.

"I had no idea this area of town was even here," Sonny said as she climbed down from the bike and pulled the helmet from her head. With just a few fluffs, her Afro was back to looking as wild and sexy as ever, suffering no ill effects from being smashed underneath the helmet.

She gestured to the quaint shops and storefronts. "This looks like something out of a Norman Rockwell painting."

"This used to be the most vibrant area in all of Maplesville, until the mall and all of those restaurants moved in. But there's a push to revitalize this part of town," Ian said. He pointed to the pharmacy. "That's the building I want to buy."

Sonny swung toward the dark brown brick

building. "I can understand why," she said. "It's beautiful. And it's the perfect location, being on the corner. You have windows all around. Perfect for—"

"—displaying the bikes," Ian said with her.

"My dad used to talk about opening up his own bike shop all the time," he continued. "This is the building he wanted. He'd say it was being wasted on selling Band-Aids and foot cream."

"So this goes beyond you just wanting to sell motorcycles. It was your dad's dream."

"It was my dad's dream first, but it soon became mine, too. I started helping him when I was five years old. I'd hand him the tools while he worked." A smile drew across Ian's lips. "I'd sit there for hours, watching him, waiting for him to need the torque wrench or seal driver. By the time I turned eight, I was working right there alongside him."

"Your face lights up when you talk about him," Sonny said.

"He was a good guy," Ian said. "The best guy."

Sonny's warm smile lit up her face. "I really hope this happens for you. If anyone deserves to have their dream come true, it's you."

He cocked his head to the side. "What makes you think I'm so deserving?"

"Because you *are*. Just look at how much you've sacrificed for your sister." She walked over to him and took him by the hand, then started a slow stroll along the sidewalk surrounding the vacant building. "I know you consider it your responsibility, but it isn't, Ian. Kimmie still has a parent who is responsible for her upbringing." She stopped walking and turned to him. She enclosed his hand in hers and gave it a delicate squeeze. "I know she appreciates you, but I hope she realizes how lucky she is to have you as a brother. That not everyone would have made the choice you made when you chose to raise her."

Ian didn't attempt to speak. The ball of emotion lodged in his throat made it impossible.

For the past four years he had not done a single thing without considering how it would impact his baby sister. His life was not his own. Everything he did, every decision he made was with Kimmie in mind. He never expected praise for doing what Ian fully believed was the only thing he *could* do, but to hear those words, to have someone acknowledge the costs he'd shouldered, meant so much more than he would have ever believed.

"Thank you," he finally said. Despite clearing his throat, the words still came out rusty.

A small smile tipped up the corner of Sonny's lips. "I figure Kimmie doesn't say it as often as she probably should. At this age everything is about her, but she knows, Ian. And she's grateful."

She stepped up to him and placed the sweetest, gentlest kiss upon his lips. Ian closed his eyes and concentrated on the smooth, supple texture of her soft mouth, committing the feeling to memory.

He took her other hand and brought both to his lips. He leaned forward, until their foreheads met above their clasped hands.

He stared into her eyes and whispered, "You have no idea how much I needed to hear that."

"Yes, I did," she whispered back. "You're a good man, Ian Landry. Despite the fact that you work too much."

"I don't—" Ian stopped short. He did spend much of his time working, either at the refinery, Trey's shop, or in his garage. "The work I do on the bikes isn't *work* work," he defended. "I actually enjoy it. What's that saying? 'Do something you enjoy and you'll never work a day in your life?'"

He pulled her to him, wrapping his arms around her waist. "If you think I work too much maybe you can help me come up with some ways to have a little fun."

"What do you have in mind?" she asked.

"How daring is your adventurous side?" Ian asked.

She released his hands and sauntered over to the motorcycle. "Why are you still standing there?"

An hour later, Ian couldn't decide what he

regretted most: ever suggesting that they take a dip in Ponderosa Pond or not suggesting that they do so sooner. He hadn't planned it. Their adventure was supposed to be a wild ride testing the limits of the Honda through the sugarcane fields on the outskirts of town. They'd come upon Ponderosa Pond and, because they were both hot and sweaty after a half hour of riding underneath the blazing sun, Ian had jokingly suggested they dive in.

He never expected Sonny to take him up on it. But, God, was he happy she had.

He'd had an impressive collection of *Playboy* magazines as a teen, but none of the glossy spreads he'd kept hidden in his closet could have prepared him for the goddess that was Madison White. There had been a moment just after she stripped down to her underwear without a care in the world that Ian honestly thought he would die. He'd stopped breathing and couldn't remember how to start pulling air back into his lungs.

He'd finally gotten control of his breathing, but had given up on trying to rein in his body's reaction to her. His hard-on was like a piece of marble, tenting his snug boxer briefs.

He lounged underneath the arching branches of a massive oak tree, leaning on one elbow, his legs stretched out in front of him. Sonny stood on a piece of a thick fallen tree trunk that hung just over the edge of the pond.

Her matching bra and panty looked as if it was painted onto her body. Ian knew he'd dream about that deep berry-colored satin and lace lingerie for countless nights to come. The way the sun shone through the leaves of the trees towering above them, casting strips of shadow and light across her flawless brown skin, made him ache for her even more.

She looked over her shoulder. "Are you ever going to get in this water?"

"Probably not," Ian said. "But you go right ahead. I'm enjoying the view."

She shook her head then dove, slicing through the water and causing subtle waves to reverberate along the water's edge. She swam out to the middle of the pond and then back to the shore.

She looked like a mythical Egyptian deity as she sauntered out of the pond, rivulets of water glistening as they trailed down her deep brown skin. She stopped a few feet away from him, braced her feet slightly apart and placed both hands on her hips.

"I thought *we* were swimming?" she said. "It doesn't count if you don't join me."

"You'd have to drag me to the water," Ian said. "I couldn't walk right now even if I tried."

She glanced down at his relentless erection and laughed. "On a scale of one-to-ten, how painful is that?"

"A thousand," he answered.

"What about your finger?"

He lifted his hand and wiggled his fingers. "It's a little sore, but not nearly as…uh…uncomfortable as this other thing."

She sat down next to him, folding her smooth legs underneath her. "It may not be as noticeable, but this is just as uncomfortable for me," Sonny said.

He released a groan as his head fell back against the grass. He covered his eyes with his forearm. "So we're both just sitting here in agony?"

"I never expected it to be so hard to fight this attraction."

"So why are we fighting it again? Don't bother answering that," Ian said. "We both know the reasons by heart."

"Is it just me, or do those reasons seem kind of flimsy when there's nothing but a couple of pieces of underwear between us? I've never been so tempted to go back on my word in my life."

Ian let out a loud groan, his arm still covering his eyes. "God, Sonny, you're killing me. Why would you say something like that when you know I forgot my wallet at home?"

He still felt like a dolt for that. She'd had to pay for their ice cream.

After a long pause, Sonny's muted voice cut through the fog of sexual frustration currently clouding his brain.

"Not everything requires a condom," she

said.

Ian's stomach tightened. He lifted his arm and peered up at her. "What are you suggesting?"

This time, her laugh was throaty. And sexy as hell.

The smile in her eyes was as naughty as the one tugging at the corners of her lips. She got on all fours, straddling his legs. When her fingers caught the waistband of his heather gray boxer briefs and tugged downward, Ian lost the ability to breathe.

"Sonny," he let out with a soft moan as his erection sprang free.

"Shhh," she admonished. "Just let me do this."

He bit the inside of his cheek to stop himself from making a sound as she positioned herself above him, dipped her head and pulled his erection into her mouth.

Ian's eyes slid closed as he concentrated on the warm feel of her mouth surrounding him. That she would even *want* to do this for him filled him with a heady mixture of desire and gratitude. His hips lifted of their own volition, moving with her mouth as she slowly swallowed his entire length. As she lifted her head she ran her tongue along the underside. Then she lowered her head again, the gentle scrape of her teeth adding just enough friction to set his entire being on fire.

"Damn," Ian grunted. His legs shook. His stomach tightened. His skin burned with the desire rushing through him.

She released him with a loud *pop* and looked up at him. "You okay up there?"

"God, Sonny" Ian groaned.

Another of those low, throaty laughs floated to his ears as she wrapped her fist around the base of his cock and pumped up and down. The collection of rings on her fingers rippled along his sensitive skin. She lowered her head again, loping her tongue around the rim of his head and then sucking the tip inside, her mouth soon moving with the same fervency as her hands. The sensation was enough to make him lose his ever-loving mind.

He felt the orgasm building deep inside, threatening to erupt any second.

"I can't…hold out…much longer," Ian husked out between pants.

She swept her tongue along the tip as her hands continued to pump. "Then don't," she whispered, her warm breath fanning across the tip of his cock.

Ian tried to hold off, but when she drew him all the way in again, he couldn't fight it. He came in violent spurts, his body jerking as it emptied inside Sonny's moist mouth.

He collapsed on the soft grass; his body replete with the kind of satisfaction he hadn't felt since the last time she had rocked his world.

No. This was better than before. That night at The Corral they were just two strangers engaged in a one-night stand. She knew him now, knew enough about him to decide how she felt about him as a person. Yet she'd still chosen to perform one of the most intimate acts two people could engage in, giving him more pleasure than he could handle.

Ian reached over and grabbed her hand. "If I told you 'I love you,' you'd think it was just the orgasm talking, wouldn't you?"

Her head flew back, her musical laughter filling the glen surrounding the pond.

"Yes, I would," she answered.

"Thought so." He swept his thumb back and forth across her skin. "I promise to reciprocate as soon as I get feeling back in my arms and legs," he said.

"It's not about reciprocating," she said.

She got on all fours again and traveled up his body, her hardened, lace-covered nipples skimming along his chest. Ian swallowed a moan.

Sonny leaned over and whispered in his ear. "Besides, it looked like you needed a stress-reliever more than I did. Did it work?"

"Hell yes," he said. He caught her arm and tugged her down, until she lay flat against him. Then he slipped his hand down between her legs, his fingers gliding over her lace-covered mound.

Sonny released a low groan. "I already told you—"

"Shhh," Ian whispered against her neck. He repeated her words back to her. "Let me do this."

As his mouth trailed along her pliant skin, his fingers skimmed the edges of the berry-colored lace shielding her sex. Ian moved the material to the side and stroked the pad of his thumb through her drenching folds. The sexy murmurs that escaped her throat only spurred him on, and when Sonny's hand wrapped around his thickening erection, Ian nearly lost it.

As she caressed him, he returned the favor, sliding his fingers back and forth against her slippery sex. He eased a first, and then a second finger inside of her, driving them in and out with quickening strokes. When his thumb swept over the bundle of nerves at her clef, Sonny clamped her thighs together, locking his arm in place.

"More," she choked out with a desperate sigh. She pumped her fist up and down his cock, squeezing every time he ground his thumb against her clit.

Ian could feel another orgasm building. His stomach clenched as the heady pleasure of his impending release started to seep into his bones. But there was no way in hell he would allow himself to climax before she did.

Levering himself up on one elbow, he

curved his fingers upward inside her, until he found the pad of rigid flesh he sought, then he pressed down. Sonny's back arched as she screamed her release. The feel of her coming apart around his fingers, her warm flesh clasping him, triggered his own climax.

Ian could barely comprehend the intensity of the pleasure that swept through him. He was stunned by the hunger, the relentless passion bursting through him. But it had to do with so much more than just a physical release. He felt it in every inch of his being; she held him spellbound.

He buried his head against her neck and concentrated on pulling air into his lungs. When he was finally able to catch his breath, Ian lifted his head and planted a kiss on Sonny's incredibly supple lips.

"We can't ignore this any longer," Ian whispered against her mouth. "It can be like this every single time, Sonny. I refuse to deny us this kind of pleasure when we both want it."

"Ian—"

The mollifying tone in her voice was exactly the opposite of what he wanted to hear.

"Don't," Ian said. "Don't mess up what just happened here by disagreeing with me. You *know* we would be good together."

"Ian, despite what we just did, we can't forget *why* we said no sex."

"Because of Kimmie?" He motioned around

them. "I don't see her around. Do you?"

"So is this your plan? We'll come out to this pond every time we want to get busy?"

"It wouldn't be that way."

"Actually, it would. You can't take me back to your place, and I can't take you back to mine, not if you don't want to give Kimmie the wrong impression. We would be sneaking around, having sex in my car or in a motel that charges by the hour. I don't want that, Ian. And not wanting to negatively influence Kimmie was *your* reason. Mine is different."

"Right," he said. "You could be gone in a couple of weeks."

"Yes," she said, her voice gentle. "I could be. You don't want to start something up with me when I may be gone soon."

Her words hit him like a cannonball to the gut. He tried not to think about her temporary status, but she'd reminded him more than once that Maplesville was only a pit stop on her journey—a place for her to gain some work experience while she figured out her next steps.

Sonny lifted herself up, then tugged his hands, pulling him into a sitting position.

"Maybe we should take today for what it was—a fun afternoon together. But I think we can both agree that it's probably better that we stick with our original plan."

She gathered his clothes from where he'd laid them out and handed them to him. Then she started putting on her own clothes. A million protests clamored inside of him, beating against his chest.

Maybe she thought it was for the best, but Ian was done with that kind of thinking. He wasn't sure how much time he had left with her, but one thing he did know is that he refused to waste what precious little time they might have fighting these feelings. It was time to go after what he wanted.

And he wanted her.

# Chapter Six

"I need more slaw!"

Sonny's voice rang out over the din of carnival noises bombarding her at every turn.

"Here it is," Kiera said, placing a huge bowl of the cabbage and carrot slaw with chipotle-lime dressing in front of her. The line outside of Kiera's Kickin' Kajun food truck had been at least twenty people deep for the past two hours, and everybody wanted the fish tacos with the special slaw. She and Kiera endured another half hour of non-stop customers before the line finally tapered off.

Sonny slumped against the stainless steel counter, thoroughly exhausted. "Am I delusional, or has every resident in Maplesville been to this truck twice already?" She blew out a breath. "I thought that line would never end."

"Welcome to the madness," Kiera said. "At least I have the truck now, which makes it a lot easier than carting everything in and out of a booth like I did before I had a mobile kitchen. Talk about a nightmare."

"So that amount of customers is normal?"

"Oh, yeah. St. Michael's Church Fair brings in people from all over the north shore, so we're feeding way more than just Maplesville's residents." She added more thinly sliced cabbage to the bowl and gave it another toss in the dressing. "We prepped as much as possible, but you can never fully prepare. And with this beautiful weather, the crowds will only grow.

"By the way, thanks for helping out today," Kiera added. "I know this isn't part of your job description, but Macy and I got our wires crossed. She'll be here around five to relieve you, hopefully sooner."

"It's no problem," Sonny said. She peered out of the Plexiglas window. "I never considered myself a church fair kind of girl, but to be honest, I'm having fun. I have to ride that Ferris wheel before the day is out. I haven't ridden one in ages."

"St. Michael's Fair is always a blast," Kiera said. "I don't care how busy we are at the food truck, when the kids' fashion show starts you have to go to the big tent. It is the most adorable thing you will see in your entire life."

Sonny thought the entire event was the most adorable thing she'd ever seen. It was everything she'd imagined a small town church fair to be, except on a much larger scale than she'd anticipated. There had to be at least two thousand people here.

Connected booths formed the perimeter of the church grounds, with games on one side and food booths on the other. Kiera usually offered a variety of items on her food truck, but this weekend they were only selling fish tacos and crawfish etouffee-stuffed egg rolls, so that the church could sell the other traditional Louisiana favorites like jambalaya, red beans and rice, and beignets.

"Hi Sonny," Tamyra Crane, who Sonny met last week while checking out the petite woman's yoga studio, waved as she walked past the truck. "Hope I see you at a class next week."

Sonny returned the wave. "I'll try to get there," she called out from the truck's window.

She'd been pleasantly surprised to find a yoga studio in a small town like Maplesville, and thrilled to learn that Tamyra offered pay-as-you-go access. Sonny had not had a gym membership in nearly a year because she couldn't find one that didn't require patrons to sign long contracts.

She wasn't sure when something like a gym membership began to feel claustrophobic, but these days she couldn't bring herself to make even the tiniest commitment. It sometimes made her wonder if she had traveled too far to the other end of the spectrum. Ironically, here in Maplesville, even though the town was small, Sonny felt as if she had room to breathe.

The most startling—and somewhat unsettling—revelation she'd had in the past couple of days was that she had yet to experience the all-consuming urge to pack up and take off to the next stop on this journey she'd embarked upon a year ago. Sonny wasn't ready to even entertain the idea of settling down in one place. Just the thought made her chest tighten in panic. But unlike previous times, when the notion of staying put crossed her mind, the panicky feeling quickly dissipated. Only a modest drum of unease remained in its place.

She wasn't even sure how to process it. She counted on that feeling of wanderlust. It guaranteed the one thing she needed the most: Freedom.

She may have become comfortable in Maplesville much more quickly than any of the other places she'd lived since she quit her residency program, but the one thing she would not allow this small town to do is compromise her freedom. She'd fought too damn hard for it, and she wasn't giving it up for anything.

"Hey, Kiera, do you mind if I take a walk around?" Sonny asked.

"Not at all." Kiera nodded. "Maybe then you won't hurt your neck looking at a certain player over there on the softball field."

Sonny opened her mouth to protest, but Kiera stopped her, holding her hand up. "Don't try to deny it. You glance toward the softball field every chance you get. It is so obvious it's not even funny. Well, it's a little funny."

"Really, you've got it all wrong," Sonny

said, her valiant attempt at denial sounding weak even to her own ears.

"Oh, honey, please. It was obvious from the first time I saw the two of you together at Trey's shop. You both were trying so hard not to notice each other that you did the exact opposite." Her lips curved in a knowing smile. "It must be really convenient, practically living in the same house." Kiera set her elbow on the counter and rested her chin on her fist. "Feel free to share whatever you deem appropriate."

"There's nothing to share." Sonny blew out a breath and glanced at her boss. "Okay, well, maybe a little," she mumbled. She covered her face with her hands and groaned. "Let me just say this. This town is too small for one-night stands."

She told Kiera about the night she first met Ian at The Corral, leaving out specific details, but offering enough for her boss to certainly catch her drift. Then she relayed her shock at discovering the next day that Ian owned the apartment she had her heart set on renting.

"I was this close to saying to hell with it and trying out another city, but I'd just had that kickass interview with you and the apartment was exactly what I was looking for. I couldn't pass it up."

"So, that's it? There's nothing going on between you and Ian?"

"We decided there were too many

complications."

"But if the chemistry is there, what's so complicated?" Kiera asked.

Sonny decided not to bring up her temporary status as a barrier to jumping into a relationship with Ian, since talk of her leaving had become a touchy subject between her and Kiera. Even though, as Sonny had pointed out, Kiera knew it was a possibility—a *probability*—when she hired her.

"Ian has his little sister to worry about," Sonny said instead. "We've decided to avoid setting the wrong example. You can imagine the kind of mixed signals it would send if Kimmie thought there was something going on between her brother and his tenant."

Kiera stared at her for a moment before she burst out laughing.

Sonny frowned. "What's so funny?"

"Honey, if you think for even a second that that little girl cannot tell that there is some serious sexual tension between you and Ian, you're both playing yourselves."

"But we've been careful not to—"

Kiera cut her off. "Kids are smart. Adults tend to forget that." She walked over to Sonny and patted her shoulder. "Take my advice, don't fight it. You'll just end up being frustrated at all the time the two of you wasted when you inevitably do get together."

"It sounds as if you're speaking from

experience. Did you and Trey waste a lot of time?"

Kiera nodded, her face becoming serious. "We wasted nearly fifteen years. Don't do what we did."

Sonny stared at her for a moment, contemplating the cautionary tone in her voice. After wasting so many years with the wrong man, she was hesitant to even think about diving into a serious relationship.

Yet, lately, the thought of her friendship with Ian not moving toward anything more than what it was caused an odd feeling to swirl around in her gut. The desire to explore the attraction that sizzled between her and Ian every time they looked at each other was so strong, Sonny wasn't sure how much longer she could fight it.

She hung her apron on the hook just left of the food truck's rear door and went out to explore. She was surprised by how many faces she recognized in the throng of people ambling around the church grounds. She wasn't sure when or even how it had happened, but somehow over the past few weeks she'd grown used to this little town. It would make leaving even harder when the time came to move on.

*But you will.*

Yes, she would. Because being tied down, even to a town as sweet and charming as Maplesville, was not part of her plan.

*But at least you can enjoy it while you're here.*

The weather could not have been more perfect for the fair. Plenty of sunshine, mild temperatures and a gentle breeze that carried the delicious smells of all the food just waiting to be sampled.

She came upon the sweets booth and nearly lost her mind at the oodles of desserts stretched out before her. Sonny loved putting together her gourmet creations, but there was nothing better than sour cream cake and sweet potato pie made by honest-to-goodness church ladies. She saw her Maw Maw Jean in every one of their faces.

A huge white tent had been erected in the middle of the grounds. There was a main stage on one end, with a short runway that jutted out from the center. Sonny now realized it was for the fashion show that she just *had* to attend.

The rows of chairs were sparsely populated as another of the gospel choirs that had been singing under the big tent throughout the morning began a hymn. Their soulful songs reminded her of those summers in west Louisiana. Her parents had never been regular churchgoers, but when she visited Maw Maw Jean they attended services every Sunday. Sonny suddenly realized she hadn't stepped foot in a church since her grandmother's funeral.

As she strolled over to where the car show was taking place, she couldn't help but think of her dad. Back before the Nobel Prize nomination, when he'd been just an average heart surgeon with normal—though still crazy busy—work hours, he loved visiting local antique and classic car shows. There was a red and white '54 Ford Fairland in pristine condition among the cars lined up in St. Michael's asphalt parking lot. He would go wild for that car.

She had her dad to thank for her VW Bug. He'd instilled that appreciation for classic automobiles in her a long time ago.

Sonny tossed all thoughts of him from her mind. Thinking about her dad and their soured relationship would kill her mood. She was at a church fair, for crying out loud. Happy thoughts should be easy to come by, right?

Heck, all she needed to think about was the softball game currently in progress toward the rear of the grounds. It was sure to inspire all manner of happy thoughts. She wasn't particularly fond of softball. It was one of the softball players who'd caught her eye. Kiera had been telling the truth. For the past hour, whenever she went over to the window to take orders, Sonny couldn't stop herself from catching a peek.

She'd spent the past three days since their motorcycle ride avoiding Ian as best she could. That afternoon near the pond had signaled a shift between them. Unlike their encounter in the parking lot of The Corral, which had been satisfying as hell, but purely physical, what transpired between them on Wednesday had gone far beyond satisfying a sexual ache. Ian had touched an emotional plane that Sonny thought she'd closed off more than a year ago.

She'd been so careful not to let anyone reach that far, but he'd reached it on the bank of that pond. He'd connected with that closely guarded part of her soul, the part she was so afraid to leave exposed.

That panicky feeling climbed up Sonny's throat whenever she thought about the look of determination on Ian's face. They'd been on the same page as far as their relationship was concerned. Simply, that there would be no relationship. But when they arrived home Wednesday night, Ian insisted they discuss what happened.

Kimmie's interruption had saved her. When the little girl came into the garage to throw in a load of laundry, Sonny had used the opportunity to go up to her apartment. She'd made sure Vanessa Chauvin had included a line in the rental agreement she signed that her boundaries must be respected, so she knew Ian wouldn't enter her apartment unless she invited him. Which she hadn't.

Thankfully, he was back to working the night shift, so by the time she arrived home from the catering company he was already at work, and vice versa. However, she couldn't avoid him today. And, honestly, she didn't want to, not after seeing him flexing on the softball field.

The absolute best was when she caught him standing with his back to her; his feet braced apart, his arms crossed over his chest. His stance caused his white t-shirt to stretch across his solid back muscles, the hem of the shirt tapering to his waist. He'd looked too sinfully good to be standing so close to a church. She'd wanted to run her hands around his waist and lean her face against his warm back. Then she wanted his clothes to disappear.

Sonny barely held in the moan that nearly escaped.

What made her think that an underwear-swimming and blowjob combo was a bright idea?

As if she needed even more memories of Ian's delectable body to torture her at night. Or every minute of the day. After their little escapade at Ponderosa Pond, her mind seemed determined to conjure the filthiest thoughts imaginable. She lived for those filthy thoughts.

There was an announcement over the loud speaker that the kids' fashion show was about to start, so she made her way to the big tent. It was standing room only by the time Sonny arrived, but it was worth standing to see the kids doing their best New-York-model strut across the stage. Kiera was right, this *was* the most adorable thing she'd ever witnessed. She wished she'd known about the show sooner. She would have tried to convince Kimmie to take part in the eleven- to thirteen-year-old category.

Once the fashion show ended all participants were awarded tickets for the carnival rides. Sonny quickly left the tent, making a beeline straight for the Ferris wheel before the line got too long.

She was halfway to the ride when Ian fell in step next to her.

"So, you were finally able to break away from the food truck, huh?" he asked.

Sonny glanced over at him and felt a sudden burst of instant happiness. It came upon her too quickly to curb it. How was he capable of affecting her mood with his mere presence?

"Yes," she answered. "But just for a little while. I don't want to leave Kiera alone in the truck for too long."

The electricity hovering between them had been there since they first met, but it had intensified ten-fold since Wednesday afternoon at Ponderosa Pond.

She waited for him to bring it up, but instead he asked, "Where are you heading?"

Sonny's shoulders wilted with relief. She wasn't up for that discussion, especially in the middle of a church fair. She pointed straight ahead to the Ferris wheel.

"On my way to my favorite ride."

Ian's steps slowed. "I don't do heights."

"It's not that high," she said. She debated for

a second before she said, "You can join me if you want to."

"On a Ferris wheel?" He stopped, shaking his head. "No way."

"Don't tell me you're scared." Sonny captured his hand and tugged, but Ian wouldn't budge. "Oh, come on. What happened to the risk taker from a couple of days ago?"

His brow cocked. "You're actually going there?"

Sonny wanted to kick herself. Heat suffused every part of her body. She'd spent the past few days doing everything she could to avoid talking about that afternoon, and there she was bringing it up.

"I thought you were trying to forget that day ever happened," Ian continued. "Since, you know, you've dodged me like I've got a bad case of the measles since Wednesday."

"I haven't necessarily been avoiding you," she lied. She'd *totally* been avoiding him. "I've just been busy."

He continued to stare at her with that I'm-not-buying-your-bullshit look on his face. Sonny couldn't blame him, she wouldn't buy that lame excuse, either.

"Can we not talk about this right now?" she asked. "Please, Ian. I just want to ride the Ferris wheel before I have to get back to Kiera's truck."

His insistent stare told Sonny that he wouldn't let her get away with shelving this issue for much longer. But she only had to fight it until the end of the month. Then she could decide whether to move out of the apartment or to leave Maplesville all together.

Finally, Ian relented. "Okay, I'll ride the Ferris wheel with you. But, I swear, if you rock the car there will be hell to pay."

"No rocking." She laughed. "I promise."

They came upon the Ferris wheel which, thankfully, didn't have a long line. She'd promised Kiera she would be back by four o'clock, which gave her a little over fifteen minutes.

Ian gestured for her to go ahead of him as they walked up the ramp and onto the ride. The carnival worker held the slightly rocking car so they could both get in. Then he raised the metal gate up, locking them in place.

"I can't believe I let you talk me into doing this," Ian said. "I should have demanded something in return."

"Like what?"

Sonny knew his answer even before his knowing gaze settled on her. He leaned over, and in a husky voice that sent goose bumps pebbling across her skin, said, "Do you really need me to answer that?"

God, no. She didn't need to hear what he would have demanded of her, but she *wanted* to hear it.

The Ferris wheel jerked into motion and Ian

nearly toppled out of the seat.

"Oh, shit," he said, his knuckles stretching his skin as he gripped the iron bar.

Sonny tried to remain quiet, but she couldn't help it. Laughter spilled forth from her mouth.

Ian's shocked glare darted toward her. "Seriously? You're making fun of me?"

"I didn't think you were serious when you said you didn't like Ferris wheels."

"Why would I lie about that? Have you seen a single episode of one of those caught on camera shows? There's always video of some carnival ride going haywire, and it's usually the Ferris wheel. Either it breaks down and people get stuck on it for hours, or one of these damn cars breaks loose and goes flying into the crowd." He cursed underneath his breath.

Despite her better judgment, Sonny scooted closer, taking care not to shake the car. She looped her arm around his and nestled against his side.

"I'm sorry for goading you into joining me," she said.

He released a sigh before he said, "I'm not." She looked up at him, her brows arching. "If I'm going to be frightened to death, I can't think of anyone else I'd rather be with before I die."

She burst out laughing again. "How can you be both morbid and sweet?"

"It's a special talent."

Chuckling, she snuggled even closer to him

as she looked out over the fairgrounds; the white peaks of the booths surrounding the grounds looking like little perfectly shaped mountains.

"It's been ages since I rode a Ferris wheel," she said, "Actually, it's been ages since I did anything fun."

"Except for this past Wednesday, right?"

Her cheeks warmed. "This past Wednesday notwithstanding. Or that Monday I first met you at The Corral."

"Look at that. I'm the highlight of your life. You hadn't even realized it."

"It would appear so, wouldn't it?" Sonny laughed. She did that so much around him.

"So, why weren't you having any fun before you came to Maplesville and discovered the magic that is me?"

"Maybe it was wrong to say that I haven't been having fun, but it just seems as if I've had more and more reasons to celebrate since coming here. My job with Kiera, for one thing. Do you know how long I've dreamed of being a pastry chef? I'm finally doing what I've been wanting to do for years. If that's not a reason to celebrate I don't know what is."

"Maybe once we're done with Kimmie's party we can come up with a way for you to mark the occasion."

She looked over at him. "Actually, I was celebrating my new job with Kiera the night we met."

Ian's eyes instantly smoldered. "In that case I think an encore is in order."

A slow warmth spread across Sonny's skin. She thought about what Kiera had said. If what her boss had said was true, that the sexual chemistry between them was apparent, even to a twelve-year-old, then what sense did it make to fight it?

Ian grabbed her hand in a vice grip. "Is it starting to go faster?"

"You really are scared," she said. She squeezed his hand. "It'll be over in a minute."

Ian didn't ease the death grip on her hand until the ride came to a safe stop at the top of the ramp. He loosened his hold, but didn't let go. Sonny wasn't inclined to let go either. Even though she knew she should. Even though she knew that every second she allowed herself to grow closer to him, it would just make it that much harder when she inevitably left.

Yet, still, she didn't let go of his hand.

They walked off the ride and started back for the booths, their clasped hands swinging gently. Sonny recognized that she was only fooling herself by pretending there was nothing happening between them, but she only had to pretend until the end of the month.

"How long are you planning to stay out here with Kiera?" Ian asked.

"Until her assistant, Macy, shows up to relieve me. She should be here in about an hour."

They arrived at the food truck, and he finally let go of her hand.

"I'm heading out," Ian said. "I need to catch a few hours sleep before I head to work. I'll see you later. Thanks for the near-heart attack."

"I was just getting your heart pumping," Sonny said.

He leaned forward and whispered in her ear. "We know from experience that you have a much better way of doing that."

Flames shot through her bloodstream. Sonny knew her face must be red as a beet. Ian confirmed it with his rich, throaty laugh.

"That blush is the best thing ever." He winked. "I'll catch you later."

She waved goodbye, pulling her bottom lip between her teeth as she watched him walk away. Sonny released a strained sigh as she tugged on the handle and opened the food truck's back door. When she walked inside, Kiera was waiting, her arms crossed over her chest, a sardonic lift to her brow.

"What?" Sonny asked defensively.

"Nothing going on between you two?" Kiera snorted. "And I married my husband for his cooking skills."

Sonny rolled her eyes even as she chuckled. She'd been lucky enough to find a job that would allow her to hone her baking skills, but to have Kiera as a boss was a bonus she'd never expected. Sonny was pretty sure this is what it would have felt like to have a big sister.

It was funny. When she was with Kimmie, it seemed as if the younger girl looked up to *her* as the big sister. She'd been in Maplesville for a few weeks, and already was beginning to feel as if she were part of a big family.

She suppressed a sigh. Leaving this place would be so much harder than she ever anticipated.

Macy arrived a half hour later, smack in the middle of the evening dinner rush. Sonny stayed on until six o'clock, because there was no way she could leave them to handle the high demand on their own. An hour later, Kiera had to practically push her out of the food truck when she offered to stay and help them with clean up.

As Sonny made her way to her car, her cellphone trilled to the sound of Mozart's Clarinet Concerto. A cluster of nervous curiosity bubbled up in her chest. There was only one person with this ringtone, and she hadn't talked to him since she'd moved to Maplesville.

She backed up against her car door and answered, "Hi Dad."

There was no *'How are things going, honey?'* There was barely even a hello.

The brief spurt of hopefulness Sonny had allowed herself to feel died a quick death. Dr. Carter White's time was much too precious to bother with banal pleasantries, not even for the daughter he had not talked to in nearly a month.

No, this call had nothing to do with her father's concern over her well-being. Sonny soon discovered that he'd only called to request that she attend a banquet where he was being honored. Had to keep up the appearance of the accomplished, overachieving White family.

*What else was new?*

"When is it?" Sonny asked.

"Next Saturday."

She grimaced. Next Saturday was Kimmie's party.

Sonny dropped her head in her hand and massaged the space between her eyes. She was so not up for this fight, but she didn't have a choice. She and Ian had worked too hard on this party. She was not disappointing him or Kimmie.

"I can't, Dad," she answered.

"This isn't a request, Madison. It's a requirement. This is important. You're expected to be there."

"I live in another state. You can't call me a week before an event and expect me to drop everything and come to Houston."

"Yes, I can," he said. "You know this banquet happens every year."

"Yeah, and last year *you* even missed it because you were at that medical conference in Vancouver. Why am I obligated to go? It's not as if I'm receiving an award."

"Madison Elise White, this is not up for debate."

Oh, he went for the full name. Well, she was not a little girl anymore. She was not dependent on his money, nor did she need the prestige attached to his name to further her career. So he could shove that award up his ass.

Sonny felt ashamed the moment the thought popped into her head. Although his persistent demands for excellence had become downright debilitating, she still loved her father. He wasn't the warmest person in the world, and he would never win top prize for most involved parent, but Sonny knew he always wanted what was best for her.

They just so happened to completely disagree on what that was.

It no longer mattered what her father wanted. She'd taken her life back, and she was not giving up control again.

"I have to go, Dad." Sonny said. "Oh, and by the way, everything is going just peachy with me. I have a great job, a great apartment, and I haven't been arrested. You should be proud."

"Goodness, Madison. I don't know what caused this change in your attitude, but I wish you would drop it," her father said. "I'll see you next weekend. Make sure you tame that hair before coming around your mother."

And then he hung up.

Sonny stood next to the car for at least five

minutes; she was too upset to trust herself behind the wheel. She took several deep breaths. She was *not* going to let him get to her, dammit!

She'd spent her entire life twisting herself into knots, studying every textbook until she could recite the material on demand, swallowing down caffeine pills with espresso chasers; trying her hardest to live up to his standards.

She'd freed herself from that life. He could no longer make demands on her.

Back in control of her emotions, Sonny got into the car and started it up.

Twenty minutes later, she pulled into the driveway next to Ian's pickup truck. She saw the lights in the garage shining through the side window. Even if Kimmie had not already told her that she was spending the night at Anesha's, Sonny would have still known it was Ian in the garage. She could hear the rhythmic thumping of hip-hop music, despite having her car windows rolled up.

*Why isn't he at work?*

"It doesn't matter. Just say goodnight and go upstairs," Sonny said to the empty car.

Grabbing her purse from where she'd stashed it underneath the passenger seat, she locked up her car and headed into the garage.

Her feet came to a halt the minute she walked through the door.

The huge bike that sat in the center of the garage was uncovered, the fluorescent lights above gleaming off the shiny chrome. Ian leaned over it. Shirtless.

*Good Lord.*

Despite seeing him damn near completely naked just a few days ago, Sonny's mouth still went dry at the sight of all that glistening sun-kissed skin. He cranked a wrench, causing the muscles in his back and shoulders to undulate. She licked her lips and swallowed back a desperate moan.

Suddenly, Ian raised his head and turned to her. He pulled a slim remote control from his back pocket and lowered the volume on the music.

"You done looking?" he asked. "Or do you need a few more minutes?"

She crossed her arms over her chest and jutted out her chin. "I was not looking."

He pointed to the bike's chrome plate. "I could see your reflection in the bike. You've been staring at me like you want to have me for breakfast." He wiped his hands on a filthy rag. "It's okay. I know I'm hot."

Busted, Sonny burst out laughing. "And cocky as hell," she said.

His grin broadened. "That, too." He tossed the rag on a side table and sauntered toward her.

"I thought you would be at work," Sonny said, keeping her arms folded across her chest. She needed the barrier.

"I called off. I have too much work left to do

on Dale's bike. I promised him I'd have it fixed by Monday."

Sonny shook her head. "You actually used up a vacation day to stay home and work on an old bike?"

"My goal is to do this full time, remember?"

"I guess that's true," she said. "So, why didn't you display your bikes at the car and bike show out at St. Michael's? It would have been a great way to pull in potential buyers."

Ian shrugged. "I never even thought about it. My dream is to see them on my own showroom floor, with spotlights shining down on them."

"What? No spinning dais in the middle with a gleaming Harley on display?"

"That's a good idea." He grinned. "I'll have to look into that."

"I get the showroom thing, but you should think about other venues, too. Places you can use right now. You could get some interest even before you open your shop."

"*If* I ever get to open the shop," he said.

"Did something happen with the loan?"

"No," he answered. "And that's the problem. I figured if they were going to approve it I would have heard something by now."

"That's not necessarily the case, Ian. These things take time."

"Except I don't have time. I can't shake this feeling that Vanessa is going to call any day now to tell me that she's listing the Miller place."

His casual shrug didn't fool Sonny for a minute. She could sense the tension in him.

"So, how'd it go once I left the fair?" Ian asked. "Did the food truck sell out of everything?"

"Just about," Sonny said. "I'm exhausted. I swear I made a thousand tacos today."

"That's a good thing. Kiera donates half of her sales to the church."

"That's what she told me. It sounds like Kiera makes it a priority to help out the community."

"A lot of the businesses do," Ian said. He leaned his backside against the worktable that was littered with various tools, and folded his arms over his chest. "Maplesville has grown quite a bit over the past few years, but it hasn't lost that sense of community that it had back when it was a small town."

Sonny joined him at the table, mimicking his pose. "So this isn't a small town?" she asked with a chuckle.

"Compared to the way it used to be?" Ian shook his head. "At one time I knew everyone in town, or at least knew their family. Not so much these days. It's hard to keep up with all of the new people moving in."

"Like me?" She playfully nudged his shoulder.

"Hey, I never said I had a problem with you

transplants," Ian said. He leaned closer, and with challenge in his brown eyes, said, "Figuring out a way to keep you here as long as possible has become one of my new goals."

His declaration caused a ribbon of panic to twist around her chest. Yet, despite his direct threat to the very thing she held most dear—her freedom—Sonny heard herself ask, "How do you plan to do that?"

He grasped her chin between his fingers. "Like this," Ian whispered against her lips before connecting his mouth with hers.

What started as an innocent peck quickly turned into her guiltiest pleasure.

Sonny cradled the back of his head in her palm, pulling him closer as she devoured his flavor. She swept her tongue inside his mouth and wanted to cry out at the sheer taste of him. Honey with a hint of spice. The warmth of his mouth, the softness of his lips, the skill in which he worked that tongue. It caused a frustrated ache to settle over her entire body.

God, she wanted him.

But she also knew she had to put a stop to him. Encouraging Ian's kiss would only make him more insistent in his pursuit to convince her to stay, and she would not allow her hormones, of all things, to dictate her future.

Sonny swept her tongue along his lips a final time before pulling back. She rested her forehead on his, her breaths coming out in erratic pants.

"Ian, we can't keep doing this," she whispered.

"You mean stopping? Yeah, I think it's stupid too."

She chuckled softly. "You know that's not what I meant."

Reluctantly, they pulled apart. Sonny settled back against the table, her breathing still unsteady as she tried to calm her rapid heartbeats.

Her cellphone, which sat face up on the table between them, trilled. She was momentarily stunned when she looked down and saw her ex-fiancé's face staring back at her on the screen. Sonny snatched the phone from the table.

Moving to the other side of the motorcycle, she whispered fiercely into the phone. "Douglas? Why are you calling me?" She hadn't heard from him since she'd called off their engagement a year ago.

"Hello to you, too, Madison."

"Hello," she bit through clenched teeth. "Now what do you want?"

"I'm calling on behalf of your father. He said you were planning to skip the banquet, and was hoping I'd have better luck talking some sense into you."

A hysterical laugh shot out of her mouth. "Is this a joke?" Sonny asked. "Are you my father's new lapdog now? Oh, wait, that's exactly what you always wanted, isn't it? You must be thrilled."

"This type of pettiness is beneath you, Madison."

"Actually, it isn't. Haven't you heard? Petty is the new black. I excel at it."

The familiar, irritated sigh that came through the phone grated her nerves. She'd been the recipient of that sigh on more occasions than she cared to remember. And the reminder of the way it made her feel, as if she were a recalcitrant child he didn't have time to deal with, just irritated her further.

This time *she* was the one who didn't have the time for this.

"I already told my father that I have prior commitments," Sonny said. "If he had any respect for my time he wouldn't give me just a week's notice. And if he has something more to say, he needs to call me himself. I don't want to hear from you again, Douglas."

Sonny ended the call and threw her head back, releasing an exasperated sigh toward the ceiling. Working in the food truck all day had her ready to collapse. Add in calls from both her father and Douglas, and suddenly Sonny was exhausted. When she lowered her head, she found Ian staring at her, his expression unreadable.

"So?" Ian asked. He gestured to her phone. "Was that your brother? A family friend?"

Sonny remained mute. She wasn't sure she could handle this conversation in her current state. She felt completely drained.

"The phone was face up," Ian added. "I noticed the picture on the screen."

Sonny took a deep breath. "No," she said. "That wasn't a family friend. That was Douglas. My fiancé."

"*Ex*-fiancé. I meant he's my ex-fiancé," Sonny said. Her shoulders shook with her exaggerated shiver. "God, I can't believe I made that mistake."

The wave of relief that pummeled Ian at the word *ex-fiancé* was as strong as the tsunami of dread that hit him when that picture of Mr. *GQ* popped up on her phone. But unease still lingered. If she wasn't used to thinking of him in the past tense yet, the guy must still be pretty fresh in her head.

"Ask your questions," Sonny said. "I know you have some."

"I do. It doesn't mean I have the right to ask them, or that you owe me any answers."

"I'll answer," she said.

Her admission made his chest grow tight. She was willing to answer his questions. That meant she was willing to let him inside, to share a bit more of herself with him.

"Okay," Ian said. He pushed himself up on the table and rubbed the worn denim covering his thighs. "How recently did your ex-fiancé earn the ex in front of his title?"

"A year ago," she said. "I still can't believe I called him my fiancé. Maybe it's because I'm tired, or because I've tried not to think about him ever since he stopped being my fiancé."

"How long were you two together?"

"Together for five years, engaged for two."

His fingers dug into his thighs. Five years was a long damn time.

"We met our first year of medical school," she continued. "We were in the same study group. I thought it was random, but later found out that Douglas cajoled his way in."

"To get closer to you?"

Sonny nodded, then shrugged. "I was flattered. I wasn't used to guys pursuing me. As I mentioned before, my teen years were pretty awkward. Douglas was smart, accomplished. Exactly the kind of guy I knew my parents would love."

An absurd amount of jealousy raced through him.

Ian wasn't naïve enough to think she hadn't had a love life before she met him. Shit, she'd picked him up in a bar and got busy with him a couple of hours later in her car. But knowing she'd been with this one guy for five years, that she'd been set to marry him, set off a toxic feeling in Ian's gut.

"Two years seems like a pretty long

engagement," he said. "Did you break up because he wouldn't stop dragging his feet?"

"Actually, I'm the one who refused to set a wedding date," she said, shocking him yet again. "I didn't love Douglas. Not the way a woman is supposed to love her future husband. I started to suspect pretty early into our relationship that the main reason he was with me is because he saw me as a stepping-stone to working with my father. I believe that was his motive all along."

"Yet you stayed with him for five years?"

"It's...complicated," she said. Then she shook her head. "Actually, no it isn't. It isn't complicated at all. Douglas was the person my parents wanted me to marry. He was my 'perfect fit.' That's how my mother referred to him."

She folded her arms over her chest and returned to the worktable, reclaiming the pose she'd held earlier.

"My mom was right. Douglas *was* the perfect fit for the person I *pretended* to be." She looked over at him. "But I'm not that person, Ian. I never was that person. It was all an act."

"I'm not really sure how a person can spend their entire life being someone they're not."

"It's amazingly easy," Sonny said. "Especially when you feel you have no other choice." She cleared her throat. "My dad is a prominent heart surgeon in Houston, although we only returned there after I graduated high school. We lived in both Switzerland and

Germany for several years. My dad was on a medical team that was nominated for the Nobel Prize in medicine."

"So he's *that* kind of prominent," Ian said.

"Yeah, he's that kind of prominent."

"And the ex? Doug?"

"No, Douglas," she said. "No nicknames for Douglas. Serious people do not have nicknames. He never called me Sonny. It was always Madison."

"He sounds like an ass."

"He's a total ass. Breaking off that engagement was the best thing I could have done. It was the first step on my journey."

"This journey of yours," Ian started. "How did it happen? How does the daughter of a world-renowned heart surgeon wind up in little old Maplesville baking cakes?"

"One day I just made the decision to go for it. I needed out," she said. Her eyelids slid closed as she shook her head. "I was so unhappy, Ian. It felt as if I was suffocating." When she opened her eyes and looked at him, Ian was floored by the blast of raw honesty staring back at him. "Then my grandmother died. That was the true catalyst. She used to tell me that when I wake up in the morning, I should have one goal: to find whatever joy the day had in store. There was no joy in my life. When she died, I decided that life was too short to spend even a single day of it being so miserable. I knew I had to make a change."

"So you chose to become a pastry chef?"

"To be honest, my job with Kiera is the first actual chef position I've held. Although, that may change soon."

Unease sparked within him. "How so?"

"I'm afraid to even talk about it." She bit her lower lip. "I'll probably jinx myself."

"Talk about what?" Ian asked.

"One of my dream jobs just became available. I know I'm not qualified yet, but I'm thinking about interviewing for it anyway."

Ian swallowed deeply, and then had to clear his throat. "What job?" he finally asked.

"Assistant pastry chef at the Windsor Court Hotel."

"The one in New Orleans?"

She nodded. "This would be such a huge leap for me, Ian. The Windsor Court is world-renowned for their high tea, and their head pastry chef is one of the top in the country. Can you imagine all I would learn?"

"It sounds like a golden opportunity."

"It's all very pie in the sky, but I got to where I am right now by taking risks. If I hadn't done so, I would be miserable and stuck working as a surgical resident in a career I hated."

Ian could barely breathe past the dread that suddenly filled his chest at the thought of her having a job interview that could potentially drag her away from Maplesville.

"So, your grandmother," he said, trying to change the subject. "Was she a pastry chef, too?"

Sonny's light laugh filled the air. "Not at all. My grandmother, Maw Maw Jean, was known as the cake lady around town. She was self-taught, never had any kind of business license or anything. She just baked all kinds of cakes and other sweets in her home kitchen. In the summers, I helped her. I always knew this is what I wanted to do. So, about a year ago I quit my residency. And I left."

Ian's head reared back with surprise.

"Wait, you quit? After all that hard work?"

She nodded. A different thread of unease wound its way around Ian's chest.

"When you said medical school didn't work out, I thought maybe you'd been cut from the program. You know, flunked out or something."

"Actually, I had the highest rating of all residents in my program."

"Yet, you just up and quit. Just like that."

She shrugged. "It was surprisingly easy once I made the decision to do it," she said. "And then once I had my first taste of freedom, I knew I would never allow myself to be bound by anything ever again."

Ian tried to swallow down the bitterness that started to climb up his throat. He didn't want to make comparisons between what Sonny had done with her medical career and what his own mother had done with her family, but how could he not? The suffocating feeling she described sounded so similar to the same thing his mother told him before she left for Paris that it was as if they'd read from the same script.

How could he trust Sonny not to pack up and leave the way his mother had? Hell, he already knew she had one foot out the door. She could very well be out of here at the end of the month.

And even if he could convince her to stay, would he always have that worry in the back of his head that she would start to feel suffocated and decide to leave? What would that do to Kimmie?

Ian had to clear his throat before he could speak. "Are you completely estranged from your parents?" he asked.

"No," she said. She gestured to her phone, which she'd placed on the table again. "As a matter of fact, my dad called today. He wants me in Houston for a banquet where he's being honored for one thing or other. I told him I couldn't go, and so he recruited backup, as if getting Douglas to call would make a difference."

"Houston isn't that far of a drive. Why aren't you going?"

"It's next weekend," she said.

Next weekend. Kimmie's party.

*Dammit.*

Ian selfishly wanted her to be here next weekend, not only because of the work they'd put into planning Kimmie's party—let's be honest, Sonny had done most of the planning, she deserved to be here to see it all come together. Even more, Ian didn't want anything reminding her of what she'd left behind. He wanted to keep her in Maplesville as long as possible, and the thought of her even sharing the same air with the ex-fiancé she'd left in Houston weighed like lead in his belly.

At the same time, Ian didn't want the gap between her and her family to widen anymore than it had already. He knew better than most the importance of keeping family together.

"Look, Sonny, I know you think you should be here for the party, but I can handle it."

She shook her head. "No. No way."

"It's not that big of a deal."

"Yes, it is," she said. "I will not miss seeing the look on Kimmie's face when we surprise her. But it's not just the party. My father has to understand that he cannot tell me to jump and expect me to ask how high. I did that for twenty-seven years, Ian. I'm done living that way." She slapped a palm to her chest. "I'm finally finding *me*. And I like what I've found."

His lips lifted in a small smile. "I like what you've found, too. It's good to know you plan to fight for you."

Yet, even as he said the words, a pall fell

over him. Ian knew she wouldn't be here for long. Not after hearing about the life she'd left behind.

This adventure she'd started was still new and fresh, but how long before she started to miss what she'd given up? He already knew her time in Maplesville was temporary. Once the novelty of this new life she'd discovered wore off, or the pressure of her family's attempt to bring her back into their prominent lifestyle became too great, she would be gone.

Maplesville was a great town, but there wasn't enough here to hold the attention of someone who'd lived all over the world, who was used to…to whatever the hell a former medical resident with a Nobel Prize-nominated father was used to. There wasn't anything he could offer Sonny that would make her consider staying in Maplesville once she decided it was time for her to leave.

It's a good thing he hadn't gotten in too far yet. Maybe it wouldn't hurt as much to pull away.

*Not too far in yet?*

Shit. He was so far in he couldn't see his way out. Watching her go would hurt like hell.

"Hey, man, you think that cue has enough chalk yet? Just go ahead and win this game so we can start another one already."

Ian looked over at Sam and then back down at the pool table, the one he'd been playing on since high school, with the quarter-size patch of green felt missing in front of the left side pocket.

Ian had a mind to hit the seven ball toward that pocket just so he could ride Sam about bringing this ratty pool table from his mom's rec room instead of buying a new one when he moved into his condo, but his heart wouldn't be in it. He didn't have a heart for much today. Ian went for the easier shot to the right corner pocket and then set his pool cue on the rim of the table.

"I'm sitting out the next one," Ian said, taking a seat on the worn leather couch, also a transplant from Sam's parents' home. His friend really needed to get his own furniture.

"You're sitting this one out?" Dale asked. "You're the one who suggested we get together."

"Dude, what's going on with you?" Sam's annoyed voice rang out.

Ian couldn't fault his friends for their frustration. He *was* the one who'd called them. He'd had a shitty shift at the refinery and didn't want to go home because he knew his night would be just as shitty. He'd been trying to distance himself from Sonny these last few days. Ian figured it was easier to detach himself now than to wait until the day she inevitably picked up and left Maplesville. He knew it would happen eventually. Hell, if she got that job in New Orleans that she was so excited about, it would likely happen in the next couple of weeks.

He rubbed his chest in an attempt to abate the ache that had taken root there Saturday night.

Ian looked over at his two friends and debated baring his soul. The three of them had been tight since junior high school, which meant nine times out of ten he already knew what their reaction would be even before he said anything. But then he bailed on the idea.

"I'm worried about the loan not coming through in time," Ian said instead. It wasn't a complete lie. He *was* nervous about the loan. "I found out today that whoever processed my paperwork got my social security number wrong when they entered my application into the system. It's going to delay things even longer."

"Damn, man," Dale said. "If you want me to, I can give Vanessa a call, ask her if she can maybe hold off on putting the building on the market?"

Ian shook his head. "I'd never ask your sister to do that. It wouldn't be fair to the Millers. Besides, Vanessa wouldn't do it anyway."

"No, she wouldn't. I just figured I'd tell you that to make you feel better."

Ian huffed out a laugh as he took a drink from the can of soda he'd grabbed from Sam's fridge when he first arrived.

His answer seemed to have satisfied both Sam and Dale, which was good, because he wasn't up to discussing Sonny with them. Not yet.

Besides, what would he say? That he was falling for his beautiful, carefree tenant? That, for a moment, he actually believed he had a chance with her? Until he'd discovered just how deeply that free-spirited attitude ran. Until he discovered that after years of committing to becoming a doctor, she'd up and quit like a kid who no longer wanted to take piano lessons—or like a mother who no longer wanted to raise her family.

His most eye-opening discovery? Learning that the bohemian goddess living above his garage came from money. Crazy money.

Here he was, crossing his fingers in hopes of getting a loan to buy a building in tiny Maplesville, while Sonny's dad owned an entire medical group in Houston with over fifty high-powered surgeons working under him. Ian still couldn't get over the shock he felt as he'd scrolled through web search results for Dr. Carter White. The man was a legend in his field. He could give his daughter the world.

What did Sonny have to gain by tying herself to a mechanic in Maplesville?

Sure, he had money coming to him in a few years from the settlement from his dad's accident, but that was what? A hundred grand? That didn't go far these days, and Ian planned to put half of that money on the side for Kimmie. Sonny probably had a trust fund ten times the size of that.

What could Ian possibly offer her? Other than a couple of orgasms in the passenger seat of her VW Bug.

He swallowed a groan.

It was so damn unfair.

But he'd never fooled himself into thinking that life was fair. Life was life. You took what it handed you and you pushed forward. Fairness wasn't guaranteed. It wasn't even expected. No one who had lost his father in a freak accident, then watched his mother checkout on her own family, could ever be naïve enough to think life was fair.

Sam tossed his pool cue on the table. "Whadda y'all say we go down to The Corral."

"I'm good with that," Dale said. "It's fifty-cent wing night."

"No!" Ian practically shouted.

Dale put both hands up. "Okay, man. Chill. I didn't realize you had something against fifty-cent wings. You don't have to eat any, you know."

Ian drew both palms down his face. "It's not the wings," he muttered.

He was seriously losing his shit, and if he didn't take it easy his friends would realize it was something more than just the bank loan. Based on the confused glances they shot his way, they already had.

But he couldn't handle The Corral tonight. Ian wasn't sure he would *ever* be able to handle it. He couldn't even drive past there without getting hard. Of course, the same was true for Ponderosa Pond, Hannah's Ice Cream Shoppe, even St. Michael's Church. It's a good thing he wasn't Catholic.

If only he could ignore the warning signals that began to blare in his head the moment he discovered Sonny had deliberately abandoned her residency program. The thought of her flunking out hadn't disturbed him nearly as much as knowing that she'd quit on her own.

He didn't want to think of her in those terms, as a quitter, as someone who could so easily walk away. He wanted her to be the kind of person who stuck around, even when things got tough.

Maybe he was being too pessimistic. Maybe, if he tried hard enough, he could convince her to stick it out. Maybe he could show her that life here with him in Maplesville is all she would ever need. He could fix bikes all day while she baked cakes, and then they could spend every night naked and sweaty in bed.

But his more practical side, the side

responsible for making sure the electric bill got paid and that the milk in the fridge wasn't expired and that his little sister flossed nightly, knew that he couldn't get caught up in this fantasy.

Sonny would eventually get tired of living in three hundred square feet of cramped space. Ian was even more convince of it after seeing the palatial Houston estate she'd grown up in displayed in one of the articles he'd run across last night.

The socialite blog had a picture of Carter White, his wife, Regina, and someone who vaguely resembled the woman currently living in the apartment above his garage. The three of them stood before the open wrought iron gates of an enormous home. Even though the caption underneath the picture stated that the younger woman was Madison White, Ian still had a hard time believing it. She had bone-straight hair, falling just past her shoulders. The dozens of bangles and the adorable nose stud were nowhere to be seen, and the white slacks and beige sweater looked like something out of a preppy catalogue. He couldn't imagine the Sonny he knew wearing something so boring without it being forced on her at gunpoint.

Worse than the dull, practical clothes, was her face. It was as beautiful as it was now, but there was something missing in her eyes. They lacked the sparkle he saw when she was working in his kitchen or flipping through fashion magazines with Kimmie. And her smile in that picture, while still lovely, was the fakest he'd ever seen.

Ian could only hope that she would never go back to that life. It became obvious to him within seconds of stumbling across that picture that the woman standing there with her parents was unhappy.

But he couldn't be sure that once she got bored she wouldn't trade in her current living situation for a brand new adventure. And if she did, the price he would pay would be far more than he was willing. Not that *he* couldn't handle a broken heart, as much as it would devastate him. He was thinking about Kimmie.

His little sister already thought Sonny hung the stars in the sky. If Kimmie thought even for a second that there was something serious between him and Sonny, that her new idol was more to their family than simply the person renting the garage apartment, she would become even more attached than she already was. And if Sonny then decided to move on?

His baby sister would be crushed.

Ian could figure out a way to deal with his broken heart, but he refused to do that to Kimmie.

The only way to prevent that from happening was to do exactly what he and Sonny had vowed to do from the very beginning. They couldn't be together. It was better for all of them.

# Chapter Seven

As he emptied a second bag of ice over the cans of soda he'd just replenished, Ian glanced over at the concession table and noticed they were running low on chips and popcorn.

Damn, at the rate these kids inhaled junk food, snacks would be appearing on some extinction list soon.

As he headed for the house, he gave the backyard a cursory glance, making sure there was no need to rough up any knuckleheaded boy Kimmie had invited to the party. So far the boys had been well behaved, but Ian knew that meant nothing. It hadn't been all that long ago that he was their age. He, Sam and Dale had been masters of being perfect gentlemen in the presence of adults, but when those adults weren't around…

Ian didn't even want to think about it. If he did he might just grab every teen boy by his collar and toss him onto the street.

Payback really was a bitch. He suddenly had the urge to apologize to the parents of every girl he'd felt up at a birthday party.

He tossed the empty soda boxes on his way into the house. When he entered the kitchen he found Sonny standing at the stove, the unique sound of popcorn popping in a metal pot ringing through the air.

"You are amazing," Ian said.

She looked over her shoulder. "I already know that. What makes me amazing this time?"

He chuckled at her sassy comeback. If he had to count all the things that made her amazing in his eyes, he would be there until next week. Yet, there he was with his hands tied, unable to do anything but fantasize about what could be if circumstances were different.

The thought made Ian want to hurl something against the wall.

"I just realized we were running low on popcorn, and here you are, already on top of it."

"My eyes have been glued to the snacks," Sonny said. "I cannot believe how much they eat! You would think they were starving."

He laughed. "Yeah, I was thinking the same thing."

Ian looked behind him to make sure they were alone, then walked up behind Sonny, slid his hand over her stomach and pressed a kiss to her neck, just underneath her ear. He did it because he had to.

And because he was a glutton for punishment.

He heard the soft sigh that escaped Sonny's lips as she relaxed against him.

"Ian," she murmured. There was a warning in her voice, but he'd be damned if there wasn't longing too. Which made this even more ridiculous.

"Yeah, I know," Ian said. "We can't do this."

It remained her favorite line where they were concerned.

He'd backed off, too, acknowledging that it was best if they not act on the attraction between them. But knowing they shouldn't didn't make it easier. Knowing they shouldn't didn't curb the urge to sweep her into his arms and pin her against the wall, especially when her skin looked so warm and dewy after standing in front of the hot stove. And when her firm backside fit so unbelievably perfect against his aching groin.

God, did he ache for her.

"Do me a favor," he whispered against her skin. "Don't pull away yet. Let me savor this for just a minute."

Instead of pulling away, which Ian half expected her to do despite his request, she brought her arms over his hand that covered her belly.

He was an idiot to put himself through this. He'd already decided that even if Sonny changed her mind, he couldn't trust her not to do exactly what his mother had done. In fact, he fully expected her to bail when she got bored with this town.

But that didn't stop Ian from wanting to pretend, just for a couple of minutes, that things were different.

"Every time I think I'm making the right decision with resisting you, you make me question it," Sonny said.

"Yeah, well, who the hell said I was going to make this easy for you?"

"Ian," she said in a strained voice.

"Shhh," Ian whispered against her skin. "I just wanted to thank you."

She turned around slightly to look over her shoulder. "For what?"

*For coming into my life.*

Even though it killed him, knowing her time with him was limited, Ian could not regret a single second of what had happened since the moment he looked down the bar at The Corral and spotted her looking back at him.

"For throwing Kimmie the best birthday party she could ever hope for," he finally answered. "I never would have been able to do this without you."

"You would have done okay by yourself," she said.

"Not even close. Every time I've looked at Kimmie today she's had this huge smile on her face. You made that smile possible. "

Sonny shut off the fire and moved the pot to another burner. Then she turned to him and cupped his cheeks in her soft hands.

"*You're* the one who made this possible. It takes an extraordinary man to go to this much trouble to make his baby sister's birthday special."

Ian's throat tightened with emotion. "Thank you," he said again, his voice hoarse.

Minutes stretched between them as they stood in the middle of the kitchen. God, how he wanted to wrap his arms around her and lose himself in her kiss.

But that wouldn't be fair to either of them.

This? Them? It wasn't going to happen. Eventually, he would accept that. Then maybe he could lay off the self-torture.

Although that probably wouldn't happen until her packed-to-the-brim VW Bug pulled out of his driveway for the very last time.

And that's when the *real* torture would begin.

"The credits are rolling," Sonny said.

"What?"

She tipped her head toward the door. "The song that's playing. It's at the end of the movie. It's time for the birthday cake. Can you help me bring it out?"

For a moment he'd forgotten there was a party in progress.

"Yeah, sure," Ian said, taking a couple of steps back. He followed her into the dining room where she'd hidden the cake she'd made at Kiera's yesterday. They each picked up one side of the rectangular base, and together carried it outside and set it on the round table Sonny had set up for it.

The crowds' excited reaction to the cake managed to put a smile on Ian's face. It looked better than it had in the picture he'd seen online.

Sonny called for everyone to gather around the table, and in the most inharmonious chorus known to mankind, they all sang happy birthday.

Because he'd apparently turned into a masochist over the last few weeks, Ian allowed himself to indulge in the fantasy of this being real. Of Sonny being here, not as the tenant renting the apartment above his garage, but as the woman at his side. *His* woman. Celebrating his little sister's birthday with him. Sharing his life.

It was a foolish dream. It would only make it that much more difficult when she left Maplesville. But he granted himself the brief fantasy all the same. He would need these memories to keep him company once she moved on.

Kimmie did the honors of cutting the first piece of cake. Ian thought it was a shame to slice through Sonny's masterpiece, but after his first bite he refused to feel bad about it. The cake was pure genius. He knew in that instant that her dream of owning her own specialty cake business would not only happen, but it would be an enormous success.

Once copious amounts of cake had been consumed by everyone, the parents of the boys who'd attended the party—none of which Ian had been forced to rough up—began to arrive. Sam and Dale, who'd both loaned Ian their pick-up trucks to serve as additional seating for the drive-in, came over, and, along with Sonny, helped to shuttle the girls to the sleepover at Michelle Foster's house.

By the time he got back home all Ian wanted to do was crash on the sofa and sleep until noon, but the backyard was a mess. He wouldn't be able to rest with trash everywhere. As he grabbed an empty garbage bag from the box underneath the sink, Ian couldn't summon the motivation to complain. Just thinking about that smile on Kimmie's face made every empty candy box and soda can strewn about the yard worth it.

He'd just wheeled the trash receptacle to the curb when he spotted Sonny's VW Bug turning onto Red Maple Drive. She pulled into the driveway. Ian was walking up to her car when she exited.

"Did I miss the clean up?" she asked. She pumped her fist in the air when he nodded. "Yes. My timing is perfect."

Ian chuckled. "It wasn't as bad as I first thought. Besides, you did enough today. I wouldn't have asked you to help."

"You know I'm only joking," she said. "I'll help clean up the kitchen."

He waved off her offer. "I'll get to it

tomorrow. It was a long day. We both deserve some downtime."

She rested her backside against the car door, her hands shoved into her front pockets. She looked so damn good Ian wanted to drop to his knees and offer himself up to her.

The air that sizzled between them was thick with want. The need to surround himself with her, to lose himself in that incredible body, was almost too much to withstand.

He told himself to look away, but his stubborn eyes refused to obey. Instead he and Sonny continued to stare at each other. She wanted him as much as he wanted her. It was right there in her eyes.

But they both had their reasons for not acting on it, and he had to remember that his reason was a damn good one. He wouldn't allow Madison White to do to his family what Yvonne Landry had done.

"This—"

"I should—"

Ian gestured for her to speak.

"I was going to say that I should probably get to bed," she opened. "Kiera and I are meeting with her sister-in-law, Jada Coleman, in the morning. They're throwing the christening party for their friend Callie's baby girl next month."

"Does that mean you'll be here at least until next month?" Ian asked. He hated hearing the hopefulness in his voice, but he also couldn't deny it.

"I, uh, I'm not sure," she said. "I haven't decided."

Her answer was like a fist to the gut.

Sonny pushed away from the car.

"Good night," she said. And then she left him standing in the middle of the driveway.

Sonny felt as if she were wading through mud as she trudged up the stairs to her apartment. She was tired to the bone, but the taxing chore of hosting over twenty preteens wasn't the only thing that had completely depleted her energy. This thing with Ian weighed as heavily as anything else.

Why was she denying herself someone she wanted so desperately?

She craved him so badly she ached with it. Her body still burned from the way he'd stared at her, his heated gaze penetrating through clothes and skin, down to the very heart of her.

This was pure insanity. What did she think would happen? Did she think shackles would magically drop from the sky and clamp down on her wrists the moment she admitted that she'd fallen for him?

But that *was* it, wasn't it? When she looked at Ian, she didn't want to leave.

That's what scared her the most. But it didn't have to be scary. It could be wonderful if she just allowed herself the freedom to explore what she'd found here with Ian.

"Just because you found him doesn't mean you have to lose yourself," Sonny whispered.

She kicked off her sandals and drew her fishnet sweater over her head, leaving her in a white tank top, dark blue jeans and bare feet. She heard the downstairs garage door open, and seconds later, the sound of footsteps pounding up the stairs.

She rushed over to the landing just in time to see Ian taking the last few steps two at a time.

"Is something wrong?" Sonny asked.

"Yes." He nodded as he rushed to her. He got right in her face and said, "Do you remember when you said you fought like hell to get what you wanted? Well, that's what I'm doing. I want you."

He grabbed both of her hands and backed her up against the wall. "And I'm not giving you up without a fight." Then he crushed his mouth to hers.

Sonny clamped her hands onto his shoulders, her legs quickly going around his waist. Ian pulled the hem of her tank from her jeans and then over her head. He buried his face against her neck, then trailed his mouth lower, nibbling the tops of her breasts where her demi-bra pushed them together, making them plump up.

Hooking her other leg around his waist, Ian carried her to the small twin bed, depositing her on the mattress and following her down.

"Tell me to stop," he said.

"No."

*"Tell me!"*

"No!" she yelled. She didn't want him to stop. She never wanted him to stop.

Ian unsnapped her jeans and slowly pulled the zipper down. Her skin burned hotter with each rasp of the metal teeth as they separated. He hooked his thumbs at her waist and pulled the denim down her hips. The snug material got caught up over her butt, eliciting a growl of frustration from Ian. He yanked the jeans down, causing Sonny to bounce on the bed.

"I'm not rushing this," he said in a voice husky with desire. "I need this to be the complete opposite of what happened at The Corral."

"Take your time," she said. "But, please, don't take too long."

He stalked up her body like a panther, trailing heated kisses along her skin. He nipped her inner thighs, sucking at the skin then licking it softly, soothingly. His index fingers hooked into the sides of her panties, and then he pulled them down her legs.

The groan that escaped Ian's throat was one of both pain and pleasure.

"No, this isn't going to be fast at all," he said. "Damn right I'm taking my time."

Sonny felt herself growing wet under the heat of his scorching gaze. He spread her legs apart and dipped his head.

The first touch of his mouth catapulted her straight to heaven. He was relentless in his pursuit, his tongue laving her folds as his fingers toyed with her opening, dipping in just slightly, before he brought his finger out and coated her sex with her own moisture. Sensation flooded her veins, delicious sparks of pleasure shooting throughout her body. Ian alternated his licks, flicking rapidly and then languidly, rolling his tongue around the tight nub of nerves at her cleft, tormenting her with every wicked touch.

Her muscles clenched when one finger finally slipped deep inside of her soaking wet sex. A desperate gasp tore from her throat and her back arched like a bow.

Sonny grew conscious of the feeling that began to build low in the pit of her belly. Her muscles tightened. Her skin grew achy. Her senses heightened as Ian closed his mouth over her clit and sucked hard.

White-hot pleasure burst through her. Her limbs shook with it, satisfaction barreling through her.

Ian levered himself up and stripped out of his clothes. Then he rolled on the condom he'd taken from his pocket before tossing his jeans aside. Sonny's mouth watered at the sight of his solid erection. She wanted that—wanted *him*—more than she wanted to escape her growing feelings for him. More than she wanted her cherished, hard-earned independence. This moment was everything to her.

Ian lowered himself over her and parted her thighs with his hips. He settled between her legs, but he didn't enter. Instead, he hovered at the entrance of her body, teasing her with the plump head of his erection.

"Ian, please," she said, rocking her hips upward, urging him on.

"In a minute," he husked. "I need to...prepare myself."

He inhaled several deep breaths before finally pushing his way inside of her. Twin moans rumbled out of their mouths. Sonny concentrated on the sensation of his thick, solid erection buried deep inside; he filled her so perfectly that it stole her breath.

Ian remained still for several heart-stopping seconds before he started to move within her. He matched her stroke for stroke, their cadence a mesmerizing rhythm as they came together in a way that made Sonny want to weep. She'd never felt so adored. Ian worshipped her body with his lovemaking, taking care in the strong, yet gentle glide of his powerful thrust. He whispered praises against her skin, his face buried against her neck as he slowly pumped in and out of her.

He braced his hands on either side of her head, the corded muscles in his arms standing out starkly on his light brown skin. The thin gold chain he wore around his neck glistened as it swung above her, in rhythm to the way his body moved.

His head dipped against her neck again, his breath gusting out in shallow pants against her moist skin. He moved faster, went deeper. Every decadent slide of his rock hard body penetrated her more fully, touching the very heart of her.

"Any second now," Ian whispered against her lips.

Sonny gripped the sheets in her fists; her entire body pulled taut as Ian's final, powerful thrust set off a million bursts of light behind her eyes.

She crashed back down to earth, her body replete with satisfaction.

"Oh, my God," Sonny breathed against his slick shoulder, holding onto him for dear life. When he started to lift off of her, she clamped her leg behind his knee, locking him in. She never wanted to let him go. Ever.

She waited for panic to attack her body at the thought of never letting him go, but there was none. What she felt right now was the complete opposite of panic. The idea of never letting Ian go, of being with him like this for as long as she possibly could, brought nothing but peace.

She drifted to sleep with the reassuring weight of Ian's body on top of her.

Sonny wasn't sure how much time had passed when her eyes popped open. Moonlight drifted through the bead curtains she'd hung over the front windows. The gentle sway created by the ceiling fan Ian must have turned on while she was sleeping made the beads' shadow dance across the bed.

"We need to talk." Ian's deep voice pierced the stillness.

Sonny twisted around so she could face him.

"Okay," she said. She could see the seriousness in his eyes reflected in the moonlight.

"We both had our reasons for holding back, but I can't do this anymore, Sonny. *We* can't do this anymore. I'm done fighting what I feel for you, and I'm done letting you fight, too."

That familiar panic returned, like the walls were closing in on her.

"Ian—"

"Don't say this was just sex," he warned. "You say it and I'm calling you a liar. This is not one-sided, Sonny."

"I know it isn't," she said. "I can't deny that I have feelings for you. There's been something between us from the very first night we met.

But—"

"But? But what?" he pressed. "But you're afraid to act on it because your parents tried to make you into something you're not? Because your ex-boyfriend used you to get closer to your dad? You're done with that part of your life, Sonny. It doesn't have anything to do with us."

"But what if it does?" she asked, shifting in the bed and holding the sheet up to her chest. "How can I be sure that I won't go right back to being that person whose entire life revolves around doing what other people want me to do?" She stared into his eyes, pleading with him to understand. "I'm finally on a path to figuring out where I want to be, *what* I want to be. I've fought too hard to get to this place in my life. I'm not giving it up."

"I'm not asking you to," he said. He captured her chin and tilted her head up ever so slightly. "No one can force you to stay. If you take that job in New Orleans or if something new comes up somewhere else, then you go. I'm not tying you down to Maplesville.

"But while you *are* here, I want to be here with you, Sonny. And not just like this," he said, gesturing between them. "I want to be here." He kissed her forehead. "And here." He dipped his head and kissed the crown of her breast, over her heart.

A chaotic mixture of fear and hope knotted in her chest. He was offering her the best of both worlds—to have him and have her freedom.

But it was never about Ian giving her permission. It was about her losing herself.

It was about her becoming too attached to one place, or to one person that she couldn't bring herself to leave, even if leaving turned out to be the best thing for her. It had been about her all along. Her decisions, her choices. *She* had always been the biggest threat to her own freedom.

And as long as she trusted herself to never lose the new person she'd found when she'd finally broken free from her former life, there shouldn't be any obstacle between her and Ian.

Yet, Sonny still couldn't bring herself to take that next step. The thought of making a commitment to him induced a shroud of panic that threatened to suffocate her.

"What if it's still too difficult for me to let you inside of my head and my heart?" she asked. "Would you still want to be here with me, even if I can't let you all the way in?"

"I would want you—expect you—to give me just as much as I plan to give you," Ian said. "I won't be in a one-sided relationship, Sonny."

"So, are you…are you giving me an ultimatum?"

"If I did that it would send you running," Ian said.

Possibly. *Probably.*

"So what are you saying?" she asked. "If I

said that I have feelings for you, but that I'm not ready to commit to anything more than what we already have, what would your response be?"

He stared at her for several long moments, the intensity in his gaze robbing the breath from her lungs.

"I would tell you that you shouldn't be afraid to open your heart to me," Ian said.

She lifted her fingers to his jaw and gently caressed it.

"And I would tell you that I need just a little more time," she said. He started to speak, but she stopped him. "Understand that I've spent the past year assuring myself that I would never do the very thing you're asking me to do, make myself vulnerable to being dependent on someone else for my happiness. I just need a little time to process this. To convince myself that I won't be in danger of losing the Sonny that I've finally found."

His strained expression told her just how much he didn't like her answer.

"How much time are we talking about?" Ian asked.

Sonny shouldn't have been caught off-guard by his question, yet she was. She'd half expected him to say "thanks, but no thanks."

And wouldn't that have made her decision so much easier?

God, who could have known that the person she found at the end of her Emancipation of

Sonny journey would be such a coward?

Yet, instead of doing the brave thing and making a decision here and now, Sonny elected to take the coward's way out.

"My lease is up in a couple of days," she said. "That would give me some time to think about what my next steps should be."

A muscle in his jaw twitched. She could see his Adam's apple bob as he swallowed deeply.

"Any time you start to question whether or not I would ever try to control you, remember tonight," he said. "This decision affects me just as much as it affects you, but I'm giving you the space you need. Someone who wants to control you would never give you what I'm giving you."

Sonny nodded, emotion clogging her throat. When she was finally able to speak, she said, "I won't forget it. Thank you, Ian. I promise, I will never forget what you've given me."

# Chapter Eight

Ian rubbed the remainder of the varnish across the slates of smooth wood, working it into the crevices, making sure every inch was evenly covered. This wasn't the type of work Trey had hired him to do, but they were running behind on this particular conversion job, so it was all hands on deck. If Trey needed him to throw on a coat of varnish, that's what he'd do.

It was just one of the reasons they all worked so well together, and one of the reasons Ian had promised Trey that he would continue to come in when he needed him, even after he opened his own bike shop.

His hand twitched as thoughts of his bike shop sent a spike of anxiety racing through his blood. Tamping down his nervousness had become today's number one pastime.

According to the voicemail Mr. Babineaux left on his phone, Ian would have a decision about the loan later today. Coming on the heels of Vanessa Chauvin's email that the Miller place was going on the market tomorrow at an asking price of $450,000, and it was a wonder he could concentrate on anything. In his head, all he could see was the neon sign for Landry

Motorcycles residing where the Miller's Pharmacy sign now hung.

He was so close to bringing his dad's dream to life. It was all just one phone call away.

"You almost done with the beadboard?" Trey called. "I can put it out to dry with the others."

"Almost," Ian called back.

As he applied more varnish to the smooth wood, his thoughts predictably drifted to Sonny. He'd given her the easy way out last night by not demanding that she make a decision about them then and there. He'd been too afraid that the decision she'd make would be the one that sent his heart crumbling to the pit of his stomach.

He'd agreed to give her time, but that didn't mean he had to sit here in limbo waiting for her to figure out what she wanted. He knew what *he* wanted. He wanted Sonny.

It was time for him to fight for what he wanted.

He gave the board one final swipe, then motioned for Trey to come and get it.

Ian wiped his hands on the rag he kept in his back pocket, then pulled his phone out to check the time. Sonny should be home from Kiera's by now. He needed to tell her that time was up.

He had become so accustomed to checking for emails from the bank or Vanessa that he clicked into his email app out of habit. His stomach pitched when he saw Mr. Babineaux's e-mail buried among the spam cluttering his inbox. The words *REGARDING YOUR LOAN* glowing like a beacon in the night.

Ian just stared at the ambiguous subject line for several seconds.

This was it.

Sparks of excitement shot up his spine as he looked at the screen, knowing that the dream he'd shared with his dad was on the cusp of becoming a reality, the start of it just one click away.

He ran a shaky hand over his mouth, letting the anticipation build just a moment longer. Then he clicked on the e-mail.

As he read the short message, everything inside him went cold.

"Hey, you okay?" Trey asked, walking up to him.

Ian swallowed, but words failed him.

"Ian?" Concern laced his boss's voice.

He shook his head and stuffed his phone in his back pocket. "I'm good," Ian said. "I just..." He let out a breath, unable to believe the words he was about to say. "I didn't get the loan."

"Aw, shit." Trey grimaced. He clamped a hand on Ian's shoulder. "I'm sorry, man."

"Well, actually I did get it, but the amount they approved won't be enough to cover the cost of the Miller place," Ian said. "Vanessa Chauvin is listing the building tomorrow at $450,000."

Trey let out a low whistle. "Pretty steep," he said. "Maybe you can work something out with the Millers directly? Come up with a payment plan? My offer still stands. You know that, don't you? Just say the word and I'll make a call."

"No," Ian shook his head.

When he'd first mentioned opening his own business, Trey's reaction had been the complete opposite of how ninety-nine percent of bosses would react. Instead of being upset about potentially losing an employee, Trey had offered to loan Ian thirty thousand dollars toward a down payment.

Ian refused it when he'd first offered, and he refused it now.

"If the bank isn't willing to give me the loan it must mean they don't think I can pay it. Why would you take that chance on me?" Ian asked.

"Sometimes you don't get the loan because banks are biased against young people just starting out," Trey said. "And I wouldn't offer it if I didn't think you were good for the money. Just take it and pay me back when you're able to get into your trust, or when you start to see a profit. This doesn't have to be a big deal."

"But it is," Ian said. "What if I take your money today and die tomorrow?"

"Would you stop the nonsense?"

"It happens. I've seen it." He snapped his fingers. "In the blink of an eye, your entire world can turn upside down."

And a seventeen year old could be thrust into a role that changes the trajectory of his entire life.

Ian ran a hand down his face. "Look, I said from the very beginning that if I didn't get the loan it just wasn't meant to be. Besides," he said, his shrug full of nonchalance he didn't feel at all. "I doubt the Miller family would be willing to work out a payment plan with me when they're bound to get offers from others who can buy the building outright."

"You really think it's going to go that quickly?"

"I know it will," Ian said. "There are a lot of companies that have had their eyes on that building for years, just waiting for it to finally go on the market. I wouldn't be surprised if it's snatched up by the end of the week."

And with it his chance to make the dream he and his dad shared a reality.

"I knew this was a possibility. I'm okay with it," Ian said, hating the taste of the lie on his tongue.

"Are you sure?" Trey asked.

He nodded because his mouth refused to form the words to tell yet another untruth. But it looked as if Trey didn't believe him anyway, not with the way his eyes narrowed as he stared at Ian.

"Why don't you knock off for the rest of the day," Trey suggested. "Mike and I can handle what's left."

It was complete bullshit. Trey needed all the help he could get, and they both knew it. But Ian took the gift he'd been offered. He could feel his attitude getting saltier by the minute. He knew the full impact of being turned down for the loan would hit him soon and he didn't need to be around anyone when that happened.

As he packed up his tools and dropped them in the toolbox he kept in the backseat of his double cab, Ian tried to decide what to do with his suddenly free afternoon. If ever there was a time to drive over to The Corral and get wasted, this was it, but Ian no longer had the luxury of being so reckless and irresponsible. He wouldn't even chance a couple of beers out at Ponderosa Pond. With his luck he'd get pulled over with the smell of alcohol on his breath and spend the night in jail.

Instead, Ian stopped in at the first convenience station he came across and bought a Dr. Pepper. Then he drove for over an hour, meandering around Maplesville, looking at all the new construction going up. All those companies had been lucky enough to have their visions financed.

His aimless driving eventually brought him to Maplesville's historic district. Ian told himself to keep driving, but he was drawn into an empty parking spot in front of Miller's Pharmacy, like his truck had magnets in the tires.

He stared at the vacant building, an ache slowly settling in his chest. It looked as if Vanessa had already been here. The red, white and blue "For Sale" sign innocently sitting in the window caused his throat to swell with emotion.

"Dammit." Ian banged his fist on the steering wheel.

He thought about taking Trey's advice and trying to work out a deal with the Millers. Between his savings and the money Trey had offered to lend him, he could give them over fifty grand as a down payment. He could say to hell with those estate taxes and bust his trust fund wide open. That would give him at least half of the money. He could try another bank. He could try *several* banks. He could get a bunch of smaller loans, cobble together the money and buy this building outright just as he'd planned. And then his dream would become a reality.

But that wasn't reality.

Reality was the bills that came every single month, bills that would need to be paid before paying back a half-dozen loans for a business that probably wouldn't turn a profit for at least the first three years. Reality was a thirteen-year-old sister who needed him. Reality was shelving his dream for a little bit longer instead of making an irrational move that could come back to bite him in the ass.

He'd gotten his first dose of reality at the age of seventeen, the day his dad was struck in the head with a falling metal pipe while slaving away at the refinery. It was the day Ian learned that no one was guaranteed an easy, straight path. Life moved sideways. It was bumpy. That day, his goals in life changed. It was all about making the path as smooth as possible for Kimmie. Her own mother had selfishly left her behind, but Ian would be damned if he did the same.

"You'll get your turn," he murmured as he started up the truck.

It may not be today, or next year, or even ten years from now, but he'd held this dream for too long to give up on it.

"I'm going to make this work, Dad," Ian said. It wouldn't be right then, but it was going to happen.

At that moment, there was another dream that Ian was determined to make a reality. The only thing blocking it was Sonny's inability to let go of her past. He was not going to allow that to get in the way of their future.

Ten minutes later he pulled into the driveway behind Sonny's VW Bug. The windows of the garage apartment were dark, but bright lights shone through his kitchen windows.

Ian entered the house through the side

kitchen door, finding Sonny and Kimmie in the kitchen, pots, pans and other remnants of a meal being prepared were everywhere.

"You're home! Guess what?" Kimmie said before Ian had the chance to speak.

So much for his no-holds-barred, lay-it-on-the-line speech to Sonny. It wasn't the type of thing he wanted to deliver with an audience.

"I'm making dinner," Kimmie continued. "And it's not frozen pizza. It's turkey meatloaf. We learned how to make it in Family and Consumer Science class and mine was the *best*."

"Family and Consumer Science?" Ian asked.

"Home Economics," Sonny explained with a grin.

He nodded. "Ah. Cool."

"I also made mashed potatoes and corn-on-the-cob, and Sonny baked cupcakes."

"She's been cooking up a storm since she got off the school bus," Sonny said. She stuck a finger full of icing in her mouth, but then the smile she wore faded. "What's wrong? You seem…off."

Ian tossed his keys on the counter. "I didn't get the loan," he said.

Sonny's face fell. "Oh, Ian." She set the bowl of icing on the counter and came over to him, wrapping her arms around his waist and burying her face against his neck. "I'm so sorry," she said, planting a kiss on his jaw. "I know how much you wanted this."

He caught her chin between his fingers and lifted her face. "Thank you," he said. His lips brushed lightly against hers, once. Twice. He went in for a third time but was stopped by a high-pitched squeal.

"OMG!"

Kimmie's eyes were as wide as the moon as she stared, mouth agape.

*Oh, great.*

"Are you two boyfriend and girlfriend?" Kimmie screeched. "Ohmigod, this is the coolest thing ever!"

Sonny twisted around, but Ian refused to let go of her. He slid both hands over her stomach, clutching her to him.

"Well, I guess that cat's finally out of the bag," Ian said.

Not as if it mattered at this point. Kimmie was going to find out sooner rather than later, because Ian was done hiding. Standing here with his arms wrapped around Sonny, drawing on the strength she'd so freely offered, it felt too damn good to let go of it.

Sonny looked up at him over her shoulder. "I guess we did a good job of sneaking around after all. It doesn't look like she had a clue."

Kimmie continued to prattle. "Anesha tried to tell me at my party, because she said the two of you were always checking each other out, but I told her she was crazy." His little sister ran up to them and threw her arms around both he and

Sonny. "This is for real, right? Like *for real* for real? Like, ohmigod, maybe you'll get *married* one day real?"

"Wait. Hold on," Ian started. He didn't want to completely freak Sonny out. It would be enough of an uphill battle to convince her to stay. But Kimmie continued to talk right over him.

"You should totally have a wedding on a beach so we can all be barefoot!" She looked to Sonny. "That's what your boss's friend, the vet lady, did. Tabitha, who's in my class, heard Dr. Webber talking about her wedding on the beach while she was giving Tabitha's hamster her shots. I do not like that hamster, but I would *love* to go to a wedding on the beach. Or you can get married in a church, I guess, but that's so boring!

"I have to text Anesha," Kimmie said. "She's going to say 'I told you so,' but, well, she did tell me. I'll let her brag this time." Kimmie raced out of the kitchen, then raced back in. She pointed to them both. "Remember, think beach wedding." Then she raced out again.

Sonny turned around to face him. Her eyes held that dazed, just got hit by Hurricane Kimmie look.

"What just happened there?" she asked.

Ian shrugged. "Kimmie happened. After an entire month, I thought you'd be used to it already."

"You'd think so." She huffed out a laugh,

then she sobered. "How are you really doing?" she asked. "I know how much you were counting on that loan."

"I would be lying if I said I wasn't disappointed," Ian admitted. "This is my dream. I'll just have to postpone it for a while longer."

"But why, Ian? Why does your dream hinge on that building? Why can't you make it happen right here? Right now?"

He shook his head. "I don't—"

"How many bikes do you have in that garage that could be sold right now?"

He squinted, thinking. "Four?" he said.

"That's your inventory. That's all you need."

"There's more to it than just the bikes."

"Sure there is, but you can think about that later. You have the bikes right now, so you have to make those work for you. You can show them around at car shows like that one at St. Michael's Church Fair. That's how you get your start. You don't need the storefront. Yes, it would have been perfect for you, but you don't always get perfect. You can do this, Ian. You can do it right now."

The excitement in her voice was infectious. The belief she had in him fed the hope suddenly racing through his veins.

He *could* do this. He could do exactly what she said. He didn't have to wait for either of his dreams to become reality. He could have everything he wanted right now.

"You're right," Ian said. "I already have everything I need. I can start small. Trey would probably let me do business out of his shop."

"And maybe you can one day convince whoever buys the Miller Pharmacy building to sell it," Sonny said. "Who knows what the future holds for you."

Ian didn't know what the future held. But he did know he wouldn't be happy if his future didn't include her.

"Sonny, I—"

The stampede-like clomp of footsteps pounding down the stairs overshadowed his words. Seconds later, Kimmie slid on the kitchen's hardwood floor a la Tom Cruise in *Risky Business*.

"Forgot this," she said. She snatched her book bag from where she'd apparently dropped it next to the pantry when she came in from school, and then she pointed to them again. "You're still thinking a beach wedding, right? Good," she said, without giving either of them the chance to answer.

Sonny laughed again. She turned back to Ian, amusement glittering in her deep brown eyes. "So, who's going to break the news to Kimmie that she's way off base?"

"Is she?" Ian asked.

He felt her stiffen and he knew he needed to make his case before she allowed those fears to take over.

He clasped his hands on her upper arms and looked her square in the eyes. "What I said to you the other night, about being okay if you left Maplesville? It's bullshit, Sonny. I'm not okay with you leaving."

"Ian, I—"

"I want you," he said. He shook his head. "No. It's more than that. I *love* you. Shit, at least I think this is love. I've never done love before. I just know that when I think of you leaving I can't breathe. You're like air to me, Sonny."

Her chest expanded with the deep breath she pulled in. "Ian, let me—"

"Tell me you don't feel something for me," he said, giving her arms a firm but gentle squeeze.

"I…I can't do that," she said, her voice a meek whisper. She looked up at him. "It would be a lie if I said I didn't."

His chest tightened. The breath stilled in his lungs.

This was it for him. This was everything. He had to make her see how good they would be together. He had to convince her to stay.

Ian ran his hands down her arms, and then he clasped both of her hands between his. He pulled her closer to him, leaning his head forward until their foreheads met.

"I had convinced myself that it was better to let you go," he said. "I told myself that it was for the best, because I thought you were exactly like my mom. But then I told you not to compare me to your ex-fiancé, so how could I continue comparing you to her? You're nothing like she is, Sonny. You didn't up and leave your old life because you just didn't want to deal with it anymore. You left because it was slowly killing you. I understand that now, and I know that you're afraid that if you stay in one place too long that it may start to slowly eat away at you, too, but it doesn't have to be that way."

He released a deep breath. "I know Maplesville is supposed to be a temporary stop on this journey for you, but I'm not ready to see this end. We haven't had a chance to start yet."

"Ian—" she started, but he cut her off again. He didn't want to hear her excuses. Didn't want to hear her reasons for wanting to leave him.

"Just tell me," Ian said, his plea desperate. "Just tell me what I have to do to convince you to stay. To give us a chance. I know you want that job in New Orleans, and I thought I'd be okay with you moving there. I figured it's only an hour away, we could see each other whenever we want to. But that's not how these things work. You'll leave and you'll be too busy with the new job and baking cakes on the side, and I'll be too busy with my work and this would end. It can't end, Sonny. It *can't*. I want you here. In this house. With me."

"It's what I want, too," she said. "This is where I want to be."

Ian reared back as if he'd been struck by lightning. He stared into her eyes, hesitant to trust the hope that stole over him. But then he grabbed at it, clung to it. In the few seconds that passed, Ian went from drowning in desperation to floating on air.

"What are you saying?" he asked.

"I backed out of the interview with the Windsor Court," she said. "I'm not ready for something on that scale. And, even if I were, I would have still backed out."

"And that means?" he asked. "I need you to spell it out for me, Sonny."

"It means that I want to be here in Maplesville with you and Kimmie." She captured his face within her palms. "I like what I've found here, Ian. I love my job with Kiera. I'm loving this town more and more every day. And…" She paused. Swallowed. "And I think I may love you, too. It scares me so much, and you're going to have to be patient with me, but I'm not ready to see this end."

"Thank God," Ian said. He grabbed her by the shoulders and brought her to his chest, holding her so tightly that he wasn't sure he would be able to let her go. He never wanted to let her go.

"I'm sorry it took me so long to realize this is what I want."

"That's okay," Ian said. "You can make up for it later."

He felt the rumble of her chuckle against his chest. Then she lifted her head, the corner of her mouth twisted up in a frown. "Now, I don't know if I'm ready to talk weddings on the beach just yet."

Ian grinned, then swallowed down the emotion clogging his throat. "I think Kimmie will get over it."

They smiled into each other's eyes and simultaneously shook their heads. "Probably not," they said at the same time.

Ian loosened his embrace, settling his clasped hands at the small of her back.

"You're sure about this?" he asked. "Not that I want you to think too much on it, but I also don't want you to feel pressured." The last thing he wanted her to do was change her mind, but he had to make sure she'd thought this through.

"Yes, I'm sure," she said.

Her next words set him at ease.

"I know exactly what I want, Ian. It's you. It's this. This is exactly where I want to be."

"Good. There's just one other thing." She looked up at him, a curious lift to her brows. "The apartment above the garage is no longer available for rent. You'll have to move in here with me."

Sonny's head flew back with her laugh. "I think I can handle that."

# Epilogue

"Are you sure you're not up for a quick trip to New York?"

Sonny lifted the natural sea sponge from the bergamot-scented bath water and squeezed it above Ian's chest, letting the sudsy water sluice down his body.

"Even if I were up for a trip to New York, I wouldn't let you get within a hundred feet of Kimmie," she said. They'd had this conversation more than once since driving Kimmie to the airport this afternoon.

"This was a stupid gift," Ian huffed. "What in the hell was I thinking? She's only thirteen. She's not old enough to spend the summer in a big city all by herself."

"She will not be by herself. She'll be surrounded by a bunch of new friends who are movie junkies like her." Sonny pressed a kiss to his temple as she glided the sponge along his chest. "This is *her* time; she doesn't need her big brother tagging along. Besides, you've got three people waiting for bikes, remember? You're in high demand, Mr. Landry. You don't have time to go traipsing around New York City. Even this bubble bath is a luxury."

"The same could be said for you," he pointed out. "The kitchen looks like an explosion in a flour factory."

"Hey, I keep a clean kitchen," Sonny said.

He had a point, though. She had more cake orders than she knew what to do with, which was just fine with her.

"I still think I should have gotten Kimmie something other than the film camp," Ian said.

Sonny let out an exaggerated sigh. "Would you stop it?" she said, slipping from behind him and maneuvering her way around the huge garden tub until she faced him. She stretched out on top of him, her breast lightly brushing his solid chest. "Stop with the worry, Ian. It was the perfect gift, for Kimmie and for you."

"For me?"

"Yes." She kissed his chin. "Because now that you don't have your little sister around to use as an excuse, you're going to live a little. It's time for you to have some fun, Ian Landry."

"I already know how to have fun. *You're* the one who was too afraid to take a ride on my motorcycle, remember?"

"Oh, I remember," she said. "I also remember that you're the one who wouldn't take a swim in the pond. I think I win."

"You do, huh?"

"Sure do," Sonny said.

"That sounds like a challenge to me. Which one of us can dish out the most fun."

Sonny raised her brow. "Honey, you'd better get ready, because I'm about to give you every bit of fun you can handle."

"Is that a promise?"

She grinned. "That's a guarantee.

Thank you so much for purchasing and reading
***All You Can Handle***.

Read the entire Moments in Maplesville series:
***A Perfect Holiday Fling*** (Callie & Stefan)
***A Little Bit Naughty*** (Jada & Mason)
***Just a Little Taste*** (Kiera & Trey)
***I Dare You!*** (Stephanie & Dustin)
***All You Can Handle*** (Sonny & Ian)
***Any Way You Want It*** (Nyree & Dale)

## The Holmes Brother Series:

Set in New Orleans, the Holmes Brothers series follows the lives of Elijah, Tobias, and Alexander Holmes as they find love in one of the world's most romantic cities.

Read ***Deliver Me, Release Me,*** and ***Rescue Me,*** available both individually and in a special bundle edition!

## In Her Wildest Dreams

Event planner Erica Cole recruits her best friend to help her plan the ultimate Valentine's Day fantasy, but chocolatier Gavin Foster is determined to show her that they should be more than just friends.

### The Rebound Guy

Relationship advisor Dexter Bryant is trying to shake his stud-for-hire image, but when Asia Carpenter makes him an offer he can't refuse, Dex will have to play the role of professional rebound guy one last time.

## Romances from Harlequin Kimani!

### The New York Sabers

*Don't miss my sizzling* ***New York Sabers*** *football series! Check my website for details!*

### Bayou Dreams

*Check out my brand new series set in the small, fictional town of Gauthier, Louisiana!*

**About the Author:**

USA Today Bestselling author Farrah Rochon hails from a small town just west of New Orleans. She has garnered much acclaim for her Holmes Brothers, New York Sabers, Bayou Dreams and Moments in Maplesville series. *I'll Catch You*, the second book in her New York Sabers series for Harlequin Kimani, was a 2012 RITA ® Award finalist. Yours Forever, the third book in the Bayou Dreams series, was a 2015 RITA® Award finalist. Farrah has been nominated for an RT BOOKReviews Reviewers Choice Award, and in 2015 received the Emma Award for Author of the Year.

When she is not writing in her favorite coffee shop, Farrah spends most of her time reading her favorite romance novels or seeing as many Broadway shows as possible. An admitted sports fanatic, Farrah feeds her addiction to football by watching New Orleans Saints games on Sunday afternoons.